THE FINAL FATE OF THE ALLIGATORS

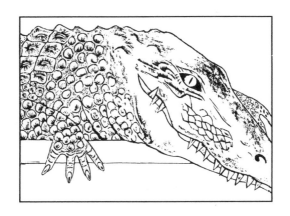

THE FINAL FATE OF THE
ALLIGATORS

STORIES FROM THE CITY

EDWARD HOAGLAND

CAPRA PRESS
SANTA BARBARA

For Joe Flaherty, John Swan, John Foley and Bill Kilduff.
Also for Molly, Mary and Amy.

Library of Congress Cataloging-in-Publication Data
Hoagland, Edward
    The final fate of the alligators / Edward Hoagland
       p. cm.
    ISBN 0-88496-341-1 : $9.95
    1. New York (N.Y.)—Fiction. I. Title.
PS3558.0334F5 1992
813'.54—dc20   91-12537
                                   CIP

CAPRA PRESS
Post Office Box 2068
Santa Barbara, CA 93120

TABLE OF CONTENTS

FOREWORD

MY ENGLISH FRIEND AARON JUDAH, raised in a mercantile family in Bombay, didn't mind me occasionally teasing him with the name "Jude the Obscure," because we were all pretty obscure. His first novel, *Clown of Bombay*, was about to come out. My second, *The Circle Home*, had just been published and had crashed in flames, as I liked to say, though total invisibility would have been a better word for it. With a few other struggling artists—a Maori painter named Ralph Hoteri, an Oregon novelist named Don Berry—we were comfortably couched under the protection of the beautiful Countess Catherine Karolyi in her little art colony in the village of Vence in the Alpes Maritimes in the south of France. When not at work, we would visit the Matisse Chapel or hike up an augerlike river canyon, past deep caves which underground springs gushed out of, past otter pools, dizzy cliffs, swimming holes, waterfalls—my wife Amy and Ralph's wife Betty enlivening the crew. I was living on the Lower East Side of New York otherwise, on $2,500 a year, as was commonly the case among writers thirty years ago, before big book contracts and university writing programs had been invented to boost their incomes. Not just the Beat spirit Seymour Krim, but Philip Roth lived on East 10th Street too. The countess was the widow of the Hungarian patriot Mihaly Karolyi, whose brief presidency in 1919 had been a beacon of democratic enlightenment between authoritarian regimes. She was vibrant, passionate, the friend or lover of Bertrand Russell, Gordon Craig and other flamboyant intellectual figures of prewar days, and now in her sixties was beloved by her large German shepherd. She lived with a middle-aged Englishwoman in this declining epoch, but had such zest that, hearing of the giddy canyons we had discovered, she galvanized herself to accompany us. And as a colony founded by a generous patroness to nurture the arts, hers was the very type of several I stayed at later, on Ossabaw Island, off Georgia, in Sweet Briar, Virginia, and at Saratoga Springs, up the Hudson River. Paying six dollars a week for a room in 1955, fifty dollars a month for a room in 1958, a hundred dollars a month for an apartment in the early 60s, I was a "low-rent" writer, in Tom Wolfe's phrase— "downwardly mobile," as Gay Talese used to kid me at publication parties—and needed a break.

But then my friend "Jude the Obscure" startled us all by fainting from hunger. He was cut from that rare category of person whom I think of as "holy fools," and whom I like to draw very close friends from. But he was a gloomier personality than my own quite standard brand of New Englander's transcendentalism, or Don Berry's Oregon frontier go-do-it energy, for that matter. He had been gloomy in India, in England and Israel, and had skipped too many meals for the sake of completing his work, and now he was starving. Ralph and Betty found him lying on his bed unconscious.

Countess Karolyi of course would soon put a stop to the hunger, and her companion, his countrywoman, I think may have succored him just as directly. She had offered to succor me also, but, being married, I had refused. Later, unmarried, I visited her in Paris and was startled all over again to discover her studio apartment decorated with paper skulls and cut-out skeletons to remind her of "how bizarrely little time I have left." Her doctor had told her that she was terminally ill.

Succor your starving artists while ye may, might be a good motto. I never saw my hunger artist again, and I'm writing of an ancient era when artists were mostly male. People knew the sculptor Mary Frank, not as *Mary Frank*, but as the photographer Robert Frank's wife, Mary—and the theatrical innovator JoAnne Akalaitis, not as *JoAnne Akalaitis,* but as the composer

Philip Glass's wife, JoAnne. Yet I've known women who comforted an array of men, ranging from Donald Barthelme to Marlon Brando, Edward Abbey to John Berryman, and never regretted it. Abbey and Berryman, red-eyed and coughing, used to look in on me on their trips to the city, and speak gratefully to bosoms opened to them, though, as always, such flings could be complicated. An old pal might throw a shoe at them too. I knew a kind-natured Playboy Playmate who owned a whole shelf of presentation copies, and bore no writer a grudge (at least in that heyday). On the other hand, a rich woman who made a practice of taking in lorn famous writers like Berryman told me she fed them according to their income level. Rich ones got steak; poor ones spaghetti. It was her pleasure, as well, when she bought a painting, to make love with the artist under it after the gallery was closed. Sadism was surely part of her thrill, and as with housing a doomed gladiator, the sense in his ardor that *We who are about to die salute you.*

This must still go on, but the milieu has changed. A youngish writer recently asked me to recommend him for a stay at the MacDowell Colony on the strength of a $300,000 advance-against-royalties he had received. He'd not previously published a book, but wanting to do a travel volume, had announced to various publishing houses that he would only set forth if he received a $200,000 advance. Now having done quite a bit better, he was seeking quarters for the winter while he wrote up his notes.

I didn't know how to reply. Great travelers, from Wilfrid Thesiger to Colin Thubron, tend to operate on a shoestring, but there is a feeling of entitlement among many new writers: budding novelists who want lifetime job tenure at a college somewhere and a Volvo in the garage. The particular angst, anguish, poverty or precarious circumstances they describe in their minimalist fiction should never be visited upon them. People quote Samuel Johnson's celebrated line that "No man but a blockhead ever wrote except for money" (though Johnson's own career refuted the idea, like his affection for the ragged genius Christopher Smart). The low-rent life of William Blake or Dostoyevsky seems absurd.

It wasn't like that as we struggled in those years—Richard Yates, Ivan Gold, Joe Flaherty, Joel Oppenheimer, George Dennison, Marge Piercy, Hayden Carruth, Frederick Exley, Galway Kinnell. During my apprenticeship in shoeleather, as I called it, which I served for the first twenty years after I got out of the army in 1957, I reached my largest audience with an essay called "The Courage of Turtles," for which I received $35. And I was glad to, because it was a newsprint audience, in *The Village Voice*, bigger than I'd had. My third novel had also crashed in invisible flames—"A Typical Example of Fictional Blight" was the *New York Times'* headline—sales of nine hundred copies after five years' work. For my next novel I shifted from ballpoint pens to using a typewriter, but that one took twenty years to do.

Meanwhile, however, I'd hit the ground running with a travel journal from British Columbia and a fluent exuberance that greased my wheels: in effect, my first essay, a form I discovered I had been made for. Like my previous books, I could recite the entire thing by heart when I was through, and like the first, I slept with it under my pillow the night the first copy arrived in the mail. But I let my hopes scud too high. When *Notes From the Century Before* scarcely received any notice in the *Times* at all and got good but scanty reviews elsewhere, what I did was go to the country to lick my wounds. They were bloody, and after licking them for a week or two, I vomited, vomited blood.

For me it ranked as an equivalent crisis to when my poor avatar, Jude the Obscure, had fainted from hunger. He'd looked for changes to institute in his life, and so did I. I'd begun teaching, for $300 per semester, at the New School for Social Research; and for $50, did book reviews for the *Herald Tribune*.

My rent by 1970 had risen to $200. I had grown up in an expensive suburb of New York, going on to prep school and Harvard—but a writer's life is leveling. My father had tried to discourage me from embarking on my career; then had asked that if I must, I use a pen name; then had written to Houghton Mifflin's attorney to ask that the publication of my first novel be stopped, arguing that it was "obscene;" and finally had pretty much cut me out of his will. So when I published stories in the *Paris Review,* the *Transatlantic Review,* the *New American Review,* it was important to me. My policy was that once they were finished, they were never allowed to spend a night at home. If they bounced back from the *Atlantic Monthly* in the morning's mail, out they went to *Harper's* that same afternoon. Even so, the boost of seeing them in print might take eighteen submissions. The very first, called "Cowboys," wound up at Saul Bellow's magazine, *The Noble Savage* (five issues, 1960-62—with Bellovian generosity, he wired me when he accepted it), which I suspect he had started in the aftermath of his anger at *The New Yorker's* rejection of his short masterpiece, "Seize the Day," which had then appeared in *Partisan Review.*

Antaeus, Witness, Pequod, New England Review, like alternative publishers such as North Point Press and *The Hungry Mind Review,* have counted for me, just as their counterparts did for so many writers I knew—Kenneth Rexroth, Gary Snyder, Craig Nova, Hilma Wolitzer, Tobias Schneebaum, Gilbert Sorrentino, Sara Vogan, John Haines, Jonathan Raban, Hortense Calisher, Wendell Berry. Raymond Carver was homeless, broke, "belly-up," as he said, when I met him, adrift, shortly before his first success, on his way to El Paso from Iowa City. Those of my friends who felt that inspiration lay partly in gin and cigarette ends (and they may have been right) didn't live quite as long, but their hardships were all of a piece with the rest of us. Buildings where the furnace caught fire or the boiler blew up, where leaks developed in the ceiling that were not fixed for endless weeks, where tenants suffering a nervous breakdown ran through the hallway wielding knives.

Does one still meet "starving" artists? Yes: a poet off an ore boat who has driven to the East Village and is being "eaten alive" by New York, he says. And regularly there are brand-name writers who need help in getting a cancer operation; regularly, young strugglers coming up—Annie Prouxl, Molly Gloss, Charlie Smith, Howard Mosher. But whether they think of their work as being improvised like a jazz riff or plotted like a piano sonata, whether they ramble through wilderness country or case the Big Apple, choose their subject matter from what they love like John McPhee, or what they hate like Joe McGinniss, "go Hollywood," or lobby for a position on a magazine's masthead, or chair an English department, writers do tend to turn bitter. In fact I can't recall ever meeting a middle-aged writer who wasn't somewhat bitter. Greeting-card and comic-book writers, thriller writers, sci-fi or sitcom writers, American Academy of Arts and Letters writers, front-page of the *New York Times Book Review* writers, sports-page or mule-train writers— in forty years in the trade I've known hundreds. The big divide seems to be between the free spirits who sit down every morning to speak their minds without first calculating the market for it, and staff writers in what I call mule trains—well-fed, nicely harnessed, with bits in their mouths and bottoms upraised for the whip of an editor—who write cover stories for *Time* or dance attendance upon the mindset of *Vanity Fair*, perhaps, on retainer.

There are talented people of my generation who devoted the meat of their careers to anticipating the tastes of *The New Yorker's* "legendary" William Shawn, with his three-year inventory of profiles and stories, all bought and paid for (oh, *would* he use yours!). The crotchets of Mr. Shawn, like those of his predecessor, Harold Ross, recounted with an anxious edge to the voice, were fodder for thousand of cocktails parties. I went to the Sudan and to Maine for Mr. Shawn ("You won't be political, will you?" he asked), and to Alaska for *Vanity Fair*'s Tina Brown (whose interest was limited to its millionaires), but in each case my attention strayed to politics and to the mountains. The price of independence is occasional despair, however. You see it in Melville, Dreiser, Hemingway, Faulkner—whoever. Bernard Malamud, among recent writers, elaborated best upon the uses to which despair can be put, like a kind of elixir at last. I remember lunches with Donald Barthelme in Greenwich Village and suppers with Hayden Carruth in Johnson, Vermont, fifteen or twenty years ago, in which each writer—separately, and at the height of his powers—expressed the belief that he was played out and about to die: like Raymond Carver "belly up," at about the same time, and Philip Roth virtually paralyzed with despondency, as he has described.

Stubborn, foolhardy, profitless writing may free one to say something new. John Updike, E.L. Doctorow, William Gaddis, Grace Paley, Paul Theroux, and Bellow have also marked me with lessons I've tried to learn—about modesty, fecundity, self-preservation, stamina, gaiety and ingenuity. The core of writing well is to tell your tale at your own pace, just as you wish, taking your chances. From the Bible to *Peter Rabbit*, that's how it's been done. We all want to strike the perfect pitch that will win us an hour's ease and aplomb, heart to heart with a million readers, fathoming their fears and their funnybones, with our own loneliness only a fortifying toxin, or sort of like how heavy hitters swing two or three bats before going to work. If the middle-aged writers I speak of had been simply bitter they would have got nothing done. An ebullient open-heartedness and mischief-making has enlivened even the most choleric ones, like John O'Hara and Edward Dahlberg.

O'Hara relished money and Dahlberg pined for it, but surely money has never meant more to authors than it does now. The smiley buzz and slippery hustle of agents, auctions, mall blitzes, talk tours, "pencil" editors verses "belly" editors (who "just do lunch"), and young writers standing around at soirées like bratpack bond salesmen comparing "scores," are a far cry from my fond hunger artist, Jude the Obscure, following his inner compass. But greed and integrity do their dance down through the ages, and in each of us. For every Kafka-pure anorexic you could cite a couple of geniuses of the fat strutting stripe of Dickens or Twain, in whom the two drives intertwined fruitfully also.

I don't see any Kafkas, Dickenses or Twains around, but who knows? Among the bohemians camped in voluntary or involuntary squalor (and they inhabited crevices of even the Eighties too), there may be a boomingly, lusciously talented soul, neurotic, fretful and bereft of hope, but churning out radiant prose. Too many writing courses are being offered, too many aspiring novelists stoop over word screens, for the number of earnest readers at large. It seems as if writing has become a therapy for loneliness, or part of the new search for solitude, like "meditation" or jogging, like Walkmans, Jacuzzis—a societal symptom, instead of an individual aptitude too pressing to ignore.

Writers are prickly, blithe, callous, and manipulative, the top-of-the-food-chain when it comes to processing other people's experiences, eavesdropping upon them, milking them of their bewilderment, happiness or grief. Tell me your story and I'll make it mine, they say. It's a higher gossip, a mixmaster process, but once in a blue moon—in Becky Sharp, Ebenezer Scrooge—the tale becomes *ours*. All the posturing, the ego-swagger, the pinched nerves that go with having writers around appear to be worth it. We willingly succor them. I've never met one who was worth reading who didn't require the mercy of patience and tact, of sympathy and a breast to cry on. And usually he or she found it.

The stories I've collected here are modest efforts from the 1960s, which was a time of personal turmoil for me. I married my first wife, got divorced quite guiltily and painfully, then remarried and had a daughter, joyfully. But my father died during the period, both to my grief and relief. Meanwhile I was experiencing the career uncertainties I've described. The freight of violence in this fiction, I would assume, is partly the result. However, throughout my childhood and adolescence, during the 1940s and 1950s, I had stuttered badly, sometimes to the point of being mute; so that may have a bearing. Stuttering seems to combine physical and emotional causes and shouldn't simply be described as a psychological disorder. But its claustrophobia, its isolating fear and searing episodes of humiliation will produce some neuroses in any case. One can speculate on the effects of stutters, leg braces and so forth upon writers who have such handicaps—the wound and the bow. I wrote about boxers, alligators, sideshow freaks, sadistic cowboys and colonels, although so did colleagues of mine who had no visible problems at all. I have included, therefore, at the end of this book an essay about violence in more general terms, which I published in *The Village Voice* in 1969.

To summarize the whats and wheres: "Cowboys" appeared in *The Noble Savage,* February, 1960. "The Last Irish Fighter" was in *Esquire* in August, 1960. "The Witness" was published in *The Paris Review,* Summer-Fall, 1967. "The Colonel's Power" was in *New American Review* in January, 1968. "Kwan's Coney Island" appeared in *New American Review* in January, 1969. "A Fable of Mammas" came out in *Transatlantic Review* in the summer of 1969. And "The Final Fate of the Alligators" was published in *The New Yorker* in October, 1969.

My own experiences inevitably entered these stories because, like Gerry Schuyler, I served for two years in the medical lab at the Valley Forge Army Hospital in Phoenixville, Pennsylvania. Later I lived at 339 Lafayette Street in Manhattan, like the "I" in "The Witness." Like Arnie Bush, I've kept pet alligators, but only small ones. I never was a cowboy or worked in a carnival, but I did work in the Ringling Brothers and Barnum & Bailey Circus for five months in 1950–51. And for several years between my two marriages, I lived at bachelorly loose ends on the Lower East Side, like Kwan, wandering boardwalk and beach at Coney Island on my days off. Many writers' best years are in the decade from age 35 to 45; and mine were soon to begin.

EDWARD HOAGLAND
Bennington, Vermont
Spring 1991

THE FINAL FATE
OF THE ALLIGATORS

I N SUCH A CROWDED, busy world the service each person per-
forms is necessarily a small one. Arnie Bush's was no exception. He was living in the Chelsea district of Manhattan at this
time, although he had lived in central California on several
occasions, as well as Chicago, and Crisfield, Maryland, and had
put in four years or more in Galveston, Texas, at a point when
he was married to a woman who lived there. He'd thought of it
as her home rather than his; all of her husbands, as far as he
knew, had left Galveston after their marriages to her ended. She
owned a laundromat and barbershop, attached, which he had
helped her manage. She was a cheerful, practical woman—
Ellen—and they'd lived with her two sons in the cottage and
patio area behind the business establishments. When he met
her, he was a merchant seaman on leave from the sea, rooming
in Galveston and hanging around the parks and bars, though he
already knew the trade of barbering also. He'd given her a
daughter, as a matter of fact—her only daughter—whom he
kept in touch with at Christmastime. The girl, whose name was
Jo-ann, had grown out of her teens by now, and he was hoping
she would visit him if she came north. He hadn't seen her since
babyhood, but when he thought of her he imagined that she
looked like her mother. Ellen was a smally built, active woman
with a bumpy complexion, a pretty figure, black, scalloped hair,
and masculine blue eyes. She carped and bitched a bit too much
but not so much you couldn't stand it, and since she wasn't as
bossy in business hours as she was at home, and since the
inescapably boring chores were handled by two colored

employees of long-standing, he had not found that the setup interrupted his independence. Instead, he'd liked being married to a businesswoman; it furnished him with the chance to operate a going concern without the ball-and-chain aspects of owning property. He hadn't married her for money reasons, however (at least, he didn't recognize the motive if he had), but for the special, jumping, bodily impetuosity between them, never equalled for him with another woman, which really never had turned sour. Just the degree of intimacy and understanding they had reached was unforgettable; he hadn't lived four years with anyone else, or given way so much, opened himself. He'd known what she was thinking when she didn't say anything, and known that underneath the peremptory manner she was a homekeeping woman as well, who didn't want to bitch at him if she did bitch, who disliked her own businesses and wanted peace and a simple household.

He had appreciated her youthful bottom, her mother's bosom, and the way she gathered her hair at the nape of her neck. They went to Matamoros together on a week's trip, leaving the kids with the woman who cooked. They dressed in sombreros and paper shirts and saw a cockfight and a festival street dance, and in his memory this trip pretty well represented what a marriage ought to be like. He had delighted in the period when she was pregnant, too, partly because his own gravity had pleased him. And Ellen had slowed down—that ambitious, scrimping fussing—had leaned on him and showed a dreamy side, as he considered, like his. More than at the chance to run the business as he wanted, he'd been happy to see her soften, see her resemble him. And the whole weighty buildup to the baby's arrival—the hydraulics, the clocking of it—had seemed the marvel that it ought to be; and then the hump under the blanket and the red head and skin, the sleeping and the sucking, the rooting, the tunneling, the reaching up, the funny-looking undershirt. He'd called her Joey Milkmouse. He'd hung over the crib: he'd brought home cotton lambs and rubber fish, full of a welling gentleness that mixed with the detachment that was native to him and easily passed for gentleness.

There were certain moments in the routines he detested—at breakfast, for example, which they hurried through. When they were about to get up from the table, she'd mention whatever was on her mind, speaking rapidly and sharply after the silence of the meal. "I want the garbage men to clean up all that stuff they're chucking on the ground; I want you to call them about it. They can't just drive away and leave a mess like that around. And the Bendix people were supposed to be here yesterday. He knows we have two machines out. They were supposed to service us on Monday and they didn't." Sometimes she felt cornered, she said, by the need to hammer at these guys and hold her own, making them do right, though she was thankful to have Bush taking over the worst of it. She wrangled with him at breakfast to get him started strong.

When she was with her kids, she didn't hold out areas of private reserve, but, having been somebody's wife already twice before, with Arnie she was a pensive, smiling chum at best, a speedy co-worker rather than the kind of ultimate companion he'd thought a wife would be. He resented it that what was a climax for him—his marriage—should be her third, and that she didn't flare up angrily, for instance, when a lady called her Mrs. Westrom, which was her previous husband's name. It reminded him of shacking up, or of an ordinary, carnally enlivened partnership, and he was disappointed, if this was marriage, even more than he admitted. He wasn't one to raise a stew about it, however; he was a quiet, self-contained fellow. Instead he paid more attention to the females in pearly slacks who huffed and puffed about the laundromat, eating weight-saver cookies and drinking coffee from the vending machines, and remembered the sea, of course, with intensifying nostalgia. He thought of his teens in Bakersfield and of the many memories of his twenties, when he had gone to sea and knocked around the world—afterward, he'd fought in Italy as an artilleryman. Except for Ellen, the baby, and his two stepsons, he had no ties to anyone, but he discovered that these ties were not indissoluble, either. The boys were runabouts, aged ten and twelve, not lonely or fazed at all, and Jo-ann was mostly Ellen's baby, or the cook's. Ellen's preoccupations were the normalities of mealtimes, meeting the mortgage bills, preserving her neighborly relationships, and seeing the children grow, whoever her husband happened to be; this was his impression anyway. She may have supposed that no husband could be held for long. She kept a bunch of photographs of herself on the coffee table and the chests of drawers to give the kids an atmosphere of family, she said. Bush, who got awfully tired of looking at them, told her she ought to go into show biz.

He was living well but was annoyed a lot. Being a believer in the rule book, a sentimentalist, he didn't like to hear her joke about their having met on the marina, as if it had been just a sort of pickup and as if she were lucky to have gotten married to the man, finally, instead of raped by him. Best were their evenings in bed, lying against the puffed pillows watching television after the kids had gone to sleep, then half an hour's succulence after lights out, and being a person of substance the next day. He was reasonable by nature; he didn't fume and fight as his restlessness increased. But it was really not a man's life there, putting in the bluing, making change. Ellen was defeatist when they quarrelled. If she let her confusion show, he was touched; if she was apprehensive, so was he; but she was unrelenting too. In the morning, she would tell him what she wanted done in the same remote, peevish tones, her face assuming the fat expression of someone drawing on inner resources. It was as if he'd as good as left her already and she had her children and friends to fall back on. Apparently, she thought her marriages were a sort of constitutional folly. She said her friends told her she was lucky to get off so lightly every time. Who these friends were Bush didn't know; he only saw a bunch of business friends—the couple at the bakery, the liquor man, the electrician. He didn't think her marriage to him had been foolish, but if that was her attitude what could he do?

He signed on the *Esso Chile* at last, and went off to Bahrein and Maracaibo. He was a wiper in the engine room; on other ships sometimes a steward. Actually, he wasn't on the sea for many years during this second stint before the grittiness and bleakness of the life drove him to land again; yet he did love the ocean and continued to talk about it wherever he was. In his own mind he was a seaman—a seaman ashore. He was nearly as lonely ashore and often thought of Ellen, suspecting, indeed, that leaving had been a mistake. He knew her show of indifference had not been real. She hadn't wanted him to go, but he'd let her pretend she didn't care. They'd been afraid; they'd both pretended it was a matter of small importance—he would go back into the merchant marine, she'd live just as before and maybe marry again. So the proof that he had made a mistake was that he hadn't stayed on the sea long. Every man made his share of mistakes. He missed being part of a household and painted her in pastel colors when he was disheartened, but he decided that it wasn't the mistakes that mattered so crucially as where you were at the end of them all.

Bush was doing fairly well. Stocky and aging, he had crewcut gray hair and a mustache and lived off Ninth Avenue, close to the harbor, keeping up with a few old nautical jokers who patronized the bars he went to. Like them, he hadn't seen much of the ocean from day to day, being hard at work or below decks in his off-hours, but what he remembered was the massive accumulation of what he'd seen. It overshadowed the other job surroundings of his younger years, just as his one marriage dominated the memories he had of other periods spent with women who for awhile had supplied him with housing and sex.

He was a sailor, he told the neighbors, and at night or on his lunch hour when he took a stroll he remembered the ocean's agitated sheen, like nobbled tin, and the majestic, chastening pitch of the water when the wind blew, the ship's joints creaking, the heavily lumbering engines, the waves thudding, making a bass hiss against the hull. His apartment, although a walk-up, wasn't too grim. One window faced south, and the sunlight wasn't impeded, because the adjacent block of tenements had been torn down—a process that he knew might pose a problem for him eventually, but in the meantime his rent was low. He had a barbering position in an uptown office building, and managed to live on his salary, saving his tips.

The alligator, like an overgrown brown invalid confined to bed, lived in the big bathtub. If an outsider had been invited in to look at it, he would have gaped, because this was no ten-inch plaything but an animal of barrel-like girth, with a rakish, pitiless mouth as long as a man's forearm and a tail as long as his legs. The cut of the mouth, however, was no clue to the alligator's mood since, like the crocodile mask that a child wears in a school play, it was vivid but never changed. The eyes, eel-gray with vertical pupils, were not as static. They seemed to have a light source within them, and the great body, scummed slightly with algae, was a battlefield shade, the shade of mud. The last time Bush had tried to determine its weight, he borrowed a slaughterhouse scale, fixed a sling, and hung the scale from a ladder, and struggled to heft the animal into place, but he couldn't get its hind end off the ground. Even so, the scale read a hundred and thirty-some pounds. He didn't name the alligator, because it wasn't human; in no way was it human. Like Headley, the fellow who had left it with him years before, he never lit on a name that sounded appropriate—not the Trinkas and Sams that apply easily to dogs. "Alligator" did very well for nomenclature, being a title that loomed in the mind, and "you" served for talking to it.

On arrival, it had still been of a size to permit it to go through the motions of swimming, drawing its arms alongside its trunk and wriggling abruptly downward into the tub until its belly brushed the bottom and its blunt snout bumped the front. It had been four feet long then, and Headley and he had carried it up to the apartment wrapped in a blanket against the cold. The fellow, who was a barfly, a lathe operator, was going south to Gainesville, Georgia, to visit his brother and wanted Bush to take care of the creature until after the holidays. He kept saying that, as big as it had grown since he had bought it—a small water lizard in a pet store—it must be worth lots of money. But he didn't show up again.

Bush laid a plank on the toilet seat and sat in the bathroom watching his new companion porpoise and wallow for exercise as best it could. Once he realized that Headley wasn't coming back, he bought a jumbo junk bathtub from a wrecking company, paying eighty-five dollars, including the delivery charge. He could shower at work, and so the inconvenience of keeping the animal was slight. Furthermore, he soon entered into what he considered an intimacy with it, so that he wouldn't have wanted to give it up. While he knew very well that alligators inhabit fresh water, having it in the apartment, he found a great many of his seaman's memories springing alive with a clarity even surpassing the clarity of life. The smoldering waves, the sharks and whales, the dull-colored, impassive seas on a smoky day—these sailors' sights and many more churned in the roil along with the alligator, who smelled, in fact, quite like the sea. He fed it on chunks of stew meat twice a week, not a demanding chore, and opened the window when the weather was warm to let in the sunlight direct.

At the public library, Bush read that alligators were mild-tempered compared to their crocodile relatives—that a man could swim in a slough populated with alligators without the likelihood of being attacked. He read that they preyed on waterfowl, muskrats, and slow-swimming fish, and he fed it a fryer chicken once in a while, bones included and the feathers left on. He fed it fish, too, always heedful enough of his overtures to its mouth end not to provoke an incident. The furor of feeding time was the main danger, when the alligator, after wringing a slab of meat like a rabbit, threw it up into the air for the pleasure of catching it deep in its throat when it came down, gargling the beef like a strong syrup. Splashing, galloping in place, it chomped and worried the meal, and Bush was touched because, after all, in such scanty quarters there weren't many satisfactions available to it. On less frenzied occasions, it liked to feel its throat rubbed, including the gums of its eighty teeth—just a long as he kept his hands off its muzzle, where the nostrils were, and away from its blistering, satin-gray eyes. The eyes sat on top of its head like two midget riders, and the nostrils collapsed and blew open like a horse's nostrils when it ducked under water.

Though the books gave a vague set of criteria, he couldn't figure out the sex of his animal. He did learn that at only five years an alligator may already be sixty-six inches, which put into perspective Headley's brief role in its life; he would have been jealous to think Headley had had it longer than him.

Except to run water into the tub, Bush often left it to its own devices. It produced a clacking sound by chopping its teeth and at eating times it grunted, too, which he assumed was some kind of adolescent version of the drumming, reverberating boom with which full-grown alligators shook the bayous. The grunt, faintly explosive, contained an animal resonance as well—a waw. At the zoo, an attendant told him that alligators rarely bred in captivity, and what he observed of conditions there assured him that he wasn't unkind to keep his at home. Like an eccentric, he didn't even regard the arrangement as strange. He was a dignified man, with a serious nose, his mustache fluffy as a Russian's, and when he got a little bit drunk nobody handled him roughly. Cutting hair every day in the week but Sunday and drinking draught beer in the evening on Twenty-third Street, he had no trouble making ends meet; and he didn't acknowledge his birthdays as landmarks at all, tucking the crimping sensation of being in his sixties into his well-knit walk. He didn't resent the gator's composure, since he himself was self-sufficient.

The alligator slipped imperceptibly toward adulthood, as befitted an animal that was created to live for a century. Its corrugated back was patterned with gray diamonds, although blurred, olive-drab colors overlaid that—not like the bright baby checks Bush saw on the specimens in the pet stores. These little ones were yellow and black and had tiny bills, with a Donald Duck ski-jump effect at the end. Their tails, though, were crenellated already and their eyes, tinted cinnamon-sulphur, were gay, iridescent, and savage.

Like a runner running a treadmill, his big friend surged in the tub, as if a birler were birling. Sometimes it inflated its lungs and then would deliberately try to submerge, swimming against its own buoyancy, until with sensuous relish it released the air and sank down. Another exercise was to seesaw, lifting and lowering its tail, making its hind legs the fulcrum—legs like afterthoughts that were tacked on. Its tail, of course, was the motive force when it swam—a walloping paddle of muscle, which the saurians of the Everglades, three times the size of his monster, swung so powerfully when they hunted at night that they could knock a drinking doe into deep water and seize her. Limber as hide, it whacked up over the edge of the tub and against the wall when the alligator wanted the sting of the blow. The tail seemed to lead a life of its own, twitching quite independently, motorized separately, and when the body moved forward, the tail, which followed after a short delay, was what lent its progress the appearance of irresistibility and crisis.

Bush provided big roasting cuts of meat now, and real mama hens. He found he was trusted more, and he could stroke the nostrils, opening and closing under his hands, or reach behind the ungainly legs to the tender, pigeon-colored armpit skin. He loved the apartment's sea smell, strong as it was, and knew that in possessing such a remarkable prize he was erasing all of that bulk of his life when he'd stayed ashore as a dreamer, working in lumberyards and snipping people's hair.

Reptile leather in the handbag shops began to be labelled "caiman," the South American relative of the alligator. Then it was gavial skin, and the baby alligators also were unobtainable; he was told they weren't being shipped any more, though his own animal, continuing to grow, seemed prepared to live on forever on behalf of the species, linked back to the dinosaur dynasty. As its girth increased, the grin on its jaws became more theoretical, as if it were pulling the wings off a barfly in its mind's eyes, while in actuality it lived like a very fat fellow, whitening like ash gradually, its eyes a white furnace. The grin wasn't precisely gloating, however, because the two corners sliced back to the very roots of its head—there was more grin, perhaps, than the gator wanted—a grin of chagrin, a grin like that worn by a man whom events have let down and who, grinning to cover the fact, betrays the bad taste at the back of his mouth.

Bush, too, grew grizzled. He read the newspapers and kept up in a less hectored fashion by hearing the headlines read on the radio—the violent malaise of the sixties, the fads and bizarreries. There was a spate of suicides in the neighborhood, and people signalled with mirrors from their bedrooms, or blinked their lights. The streets were tight with pedestrians. He made his home his castle and used binoculars to keep in touch with his neighbors, though he was not himself overswept by the claustrophobia abroad in the world, being accustomed to shipboard conditions. He watched the buildings smoking, and then when the city stopped them from smoking for the sake of the air, that in a way was eerie, too, because so much was going on inside, you knew they ought to be smoking.

The alligator had been ill only twice, when it seemed unable to open its eyes and the eyelids turned blue. It lay with its long maw closed, and a fixed vaudeville smile, propping its head on the side of the tub so that it needn't come up for air. Bush poured bouillon into its mouth through a tube and furnished heaters, and for the time that the illness lasted he didn't attempt to exercise it. Ordinarily, hauling, assisting, he got it out onto the floor every couple of days for a walk and to let it dry thoroughly—let it lie flat, sprawling its arms, while he cleaned the interstices of its skin where fungi might gather. The logistics were not ideal, but the business was very brotherly—the struggle, shoulder to shoulder, to jimmy the heavy body out of the tub—and he didn't get tired of rubbing his hands across the rich hide. On both occasions, the alligator had got well in a week or so. There were some gradual changes, though. Whereas before when he watched the beast's clumsy galumphing he had imagined the alligators in the swamps in their glory, now he began to see his friend just trying to stay alive. The alligator stared at him through its cruel pupils which contained all the harshness of millenniums past—and he wasn't so sure it was going to outlive him. A man downstairs kept fish, and Bush arranged that if he should die this person would telephone the zoo and get them to take the alligator safely. Since he wasn't made to last for a century, he hadn't expected that he might outlive his friend.

Besides the problems of fresh air and space, there was the elaborate question of diet. How could he duplicate the crunchy, glittery nutrients of a jungle river? Of course finally he couldn't—not with powdered Vitamin D and not with steer beef. Sometimes the alligator loped like an otter with constipation, humped awkwardly, and when that happened his own belly ached. These seizures disturbed him dreadfully, especially when he decided they were the result of a deficiency, and one he couldn't correct. Dancing like a bear that had burned its feet, the creature suffered sadly, though its mask was still heavy and comic and rigid. Great gouts of gas came up in bubbles, released from the alligator's digestive tract after much lurching and shuffling. It craned its neck to persuade them to come, after doing an agonized gandy dance, or a dance of death.

During the night one weekend, at last, it died. Bush didn't discover the fact until midmorning, because its position underwater was painless-looking and natural, the head floating just in the attitude of an alligator at peace with itself; he only noticed that it was dead when he saw that it didn't come up to breathe. However, the expression was a terrible one. The expression was like the Angel of Death's, if, as seemed likely, an alligator confronts the Angel of Death with the expression of the Angel of Death. And all of those aeons were etched on the mask—all of the meals in the bubbling mud, the procession of species extinguished, the mountain-building, the flooding seas and the baking sun. The framework of daily courtesies was over between them, and the fury and barbarism photographed on the face were alive like a flame.

He might have called the leather-toolers, but didn't. He and his neighbor who kept fish got help and carried the alligator down to the street late Sunday night, leaving it stretched in solitary magnificence across the sidewalk for the city to figure out what to do with.

He had these three memories, then: the sea, the few years in Texas, and the years on Twenty-first Street, with the mumbo-jumbo that filled in between.

THE COLONEL'S POWER

G ERRY SCHUYLER'S TECHNIQUE with the officers was the soft
voice, since the soft voice, of course, was a gentleman's
voice and if they were being loud the roles were reversed. It was
the peacetime army and they didn't want that. Except for the
barracks end of the life, he seldom had dealings with officious
types. His were in the Medical Service Corps, Gerry having the
plushy job of running the hospital morgue, which was seldom
in official use and most of the time was his private apartment,
where he kept his civilian clothes and whiled away hours that he
otherwise would have had to spend in more hectic surroundings. Of the four rooms, two were storerooms unconnected
with death, so he locked off the rest. He was personable and
quick, with a cocked-head approach to the world he was in,
expecting to become a lawyer. He enjoyed the lawyer's
egalitarian eye, the apprentice cynic's, and was relaxed and
responsive with his fellow privates, respectful and friendly
enough to the sergeants, and got along with the colonel, a most
subtle man with a face like a doge, a pill-taker and amateur
sphinx, quite paranoid. After an inadvertent affront to him,
there were about three hours before the misunderstanding could
not be explained away, but Gerry was just sufficiently quirky
himself to be able to spot these emergencies.

The colonel had a master's degree as a chemist-virologist and
a sense of humor about doctors, an intimate knowledge of how
they were. He came from Florida and was on his way toward
thirty years in the army now, uncertain whether he oughtn't to
quit, letting the extra pension rights go. His one great mistake
had been a disastrous quarrel with his professor at Duke as a
young man, after which he had left in a sulk without starting a

29

more rewarding career. He believed in wearing a smile, and he liked to do double takes, show surprise, and appreciated the comforts of life such as soft beds and round slumpy shoulders. His handwriting looked like debris but his clothing was smooth and casual, never exactly khaki. He bought the off-shades available to officers, either a summery-looking tan or a rich business-suit ochre. He had an acute, ironist's face with jug-handle ears and open, unmilitary eyes, which he turned to one side as he spoke, as if slightly shocked at the stories he told—wonderful childhood stories built up with the fancifying talent of a Southerner, about pigs, dogs, and Negroes called Brother Something-or-other. Ordinarily he was all gaiety and games on rainy days or when circumstances were gloomy, as if he were feeling less lonely. Then his fur rose as the weather improved.

Combined with these qualities was a cruel streak, however, which put fallen favorites to work transplanting meningitis. It became a refrain with him—"There's plenty of virus work, Private!"—so that the draftees regarded keeping one jump ahead of friction with the colonel as almost a matter of life and death. That year he happened to chair the Court-martial Board as well, and, while probably no outright miscarriages of justice occurred, when he would come back saying that the prisoner had cried, he was contemptuously pleased. Gerry in a gingerly way argued with him, wondering if, sooner or later, his decisions could help being affected by his attitude. Besides the thefts and AWOLs, another board he sat on considered unsuitability discharges, such as the WAC clerk who gave herself shocks with an electrical gizmo in order to cure her acne, or the corporal who hid in the chaplain's closet.

"I asked him why he didn't take some pills if he felt like that, instead of hiding in the closet. He said he couldn't swallow pills."

"So? If he couldn't swallow them he couldn't swallow them."

"Well, he could take them in water; he could have dissolved them. Or he could chew them," the colonel laughed. "It's a sign of mental trouble not to be able to swallow pills."

"That's what the hearing was all about, wasn't it?"

"Sure. We're letting him out. Don't worry about him. He must be already packing." He imitated giddy packing, although he wasn't nearly as reluctant to grant these releases as were the less intelligent officers. In fact, he was one of the least "chicken" officers around, the liveliest, the cleverest, who cared nothing about salutes, detested swagger, and who, though he was shy in the outside world, was conversant with it—went to recitals and plays and belonged to a club up in New York. He corresponded with German professors he'd met on his duty tours there, and directed the Officers' Quarters with a silken hand. The general got him to host dignitaries, since he knew how, but afterwards he passed blank little weekends alone on the post. His happiest days were the working weekdays, yet the doctors who used his facilities drew distinctions between him and them. He didn't especially take to them either, with their mockery of the army at the same time as they were enjoying status in it. He liked to propose dirty deals for the enlisted men, which he had no intention of carrying out, in order to see them disapprove.

With the sergeants, too, Colonel Wetthall was intricate. For instance, Sgt. Washburn, who loathed blood, was assigned to the vein-sticking room every so often, where she cried and cried. She was enormously fond of him, the main man in her life. The two of them worked cheerfully side by side much of the time. He teased her by calling her Sergeant Wash-born, imitating a mountain girl's speech and then shifting to his manorial smile. He liked functioning on a par with his peppily IQed draftees still more. Digs at the legal profession, or "What now? What's new?" he would say when Gerry appeared, wanting an answer he didn't expect. He'd gather the whole crew to watch him mix media syrup, and then swing around to ask why the floor hadn't been buffed. "Haven't had time?" he said, so that they couldn't tell if he was agreeing or ironic. Because of the colonel's changeableness the under-officers treated everybody with caution, and the sergeants, like humble technicians, weren't formidable unless someone twisted their tails. Sfc. Reynolds, the administrative sergeant, was a self-propelled man from a starved coal town who allowed himself the pleasure of questioning the college boys when they wanted a pass but otherwise, strict and fair, held himself back.

The few privates were tender as mothers from the emotionalisms of stress—a sort of a breakneck golden rule— and knew each other's every heartbeat, lavish like men with high hopes on a raft. Two were displaced druggists, one was a dentistry school dropout from Hawaii, one was a fabrics designer from Newark, and one was a playground director from the tough Bronx. In the barracks Fallon, the playground director, had the bed next to Gerry's. He was a dreamy, competent boy who let his sly jaw down to laugh and got along peacefully with the wildest types, as at home. He was serious rather than kidding, and his ambition was to build a boat patterned after a late-nineteenth century sloop whose owner had sailed around the world.

Gerry's girl situation was probably still for the record as much as for real, but he had a fine girl named Babs Babineau, a Vermont French Canadian. The colonel frowned slightly because her last boyfriend had been a Nisei, but Babs was a practical, nurse-like girl, doing X-rays, with lovely hair and a graceful shrug. Her prim face lighted when she was at ease, or particularly if she was told she was pretty. Though she was ashamed of being in the army, it had been a good move away from her home. She was stiff-upper-lip and misfortune-prone, with a thin-mouthed smile, even, square teeth, a trick knee, a shallow asthmatic's cough. She underdressed for the cold and if she took something hot in her mouth would insist upon sweating with it, not spitting it out. She turned their walks in the country into endurance tests and had a sharp hungry whine like a child set upon. Nevertheless, she was a sweetie, as dependable as she was obstinate. "She? Who's 'she,' the cat's mother?" Babs exclaimed, if Gerry neglected to introduce her around.

Terribly grateful, he lolloped affection on her, and loved the curve she curled in when she read in his rooms, her nylons glinting like two snakeskins, or seeing her come toward him at a distance, with a lean lonely beauty unaware of itself, and lift her arms quickly to him. Escaping that monotonous city sarcasm was also fun—to be able to say, "Aren't you glad you're with me?" and have Bab's reliable "yes." But such a drab life she'd been brought up to look for: says one must make the best of one's lot in the world, that grim brand of puritanism that thinks everything given away is gone.

"If you're trying to remold me, why do you bother? Why don't you grab yourself somebody else?" she said.

Gerry asked the colonel about menstruation, grinning as if he had reasons why he needed to know.

"They used to say it's the uterus weeping for its eggs. The egg that's been waiting gives up hope. It gets flushed out in a rush of tears—if that's not too old-fashioned for you," Wetthall said.

"So it means that it's over?"

"The cycle is over for the moment, yes." He looked at Gerry in a flat, placid mood. Yet the same day the department was racked neurotically by a quarrel between him and Sfc. Reynolds, of all unlikely people, the basis silly whatever it was, in which Reynolds threatened to let his enlistment lapse at the end of his hitch and the colonel, snickering softly, told him he had enough time left anyway to be shipped off to Germany next week and not see his wife and kids for two years. "Do you want it?"

The sergeant's face swelled. He shook his head.

Gerry was an optimist. Peppiness rather than a lack of grades had veered him into the service before law school, a decision he now regretted, but in the meantime he nourished his hopes on vague chattered pledges of deals someday with other excited young men on the make. And because of his summers spent traveling, he could tell what states the rest of the soldiers came from, often having been to the very town. Since he had crossed on all the big highways, a simple map of America contained marvelous clumps of impressions for him. He was right on the fence in his pleasures, not having lost as yet the sort of immediacies he'd had in his teens. For example, he had a sixth sense, so that visitors never walked in on him unawares and he scarcely troubled to look left and right before crossing a street. He didn't trip in the dark or bump into people when going around a corner. He was full of impulses he trusted. Once he got used to the dirty work, he didn't anticipate that the bodies would play any role in the cozy householder's setup that he had arranged, because they were autopsied quickly, averaging just one a week. But sometimes they'd suddenly descend, like absentee owners; and couldn't be shunted off. Most patients died at night. If they survived the sunrise, they usually pulled through until the next night. Births also occurred then, because of the same corporeal relaxation, and he was sent stillborn babies. Oddly enough, they were easier to handle than the adults, being too small and too rudimentary to have achieved human dimensions. He was sad without so much empathy, as if with a cocker spaniel.

A master sergeant in the surgical ward happened to die the same night as two soldiers who cracked up on the turnpike, and Gerry's locked-off icebox rebroadcast its claims with a vengeance, everything baying and hollering. The nurses wheeled down the lung case, all cleaned up and stoppered, the thumbs tied together and the penis tied off, but the MPs, an hour later, pounded on the door with their flashlights as if war had started and hurried the casualties in with a curse. They were bruiser MPs, rough for a hospital because of the mental wing whose escapees they had to run down, and the bodies were ghastly, long, spattered things. An amazing deadweight spread over the whole instead of being centered, as with a living man. There weren't wounds, only holes, like a stained diagram. The face of the soldier who hadn't been driving was peremptory, drawing back—look out!—with a short plaintive nose. His friend wore a grimace as if he were hearing a brutal joke, and still groped for the wheel, which he had lost. Perhaps he showed some satisfaction too, because this time he had done it up brown. Despite the need to hose and scrub, despite these coarse, arrested expressions, and despite the age-sympathy that Gerry felt, the two young privates were a relief to wrestle with, after the old chest patient who looked so shriveled and mauled, so systematically readied for death, and now had on an ambiguous smile.

None of the bodies was stiff. They were just heavy, although they became more stubborn and stone-like as time went on. After a day or two they appeared to steel themselves, turning a granite color, in order to bear the hauling which they were being subjected to. And they were either all there or else not there at all, larger than life or else insignificant, like a pile of wood shavings under a sheet. A few stocky men were inexplicably light, but a Fort Dix drillmaster with a big barrel frame bulked up like a giant compared to a wasted, frail brigadier general Gerry examined the same day, who sported a harmless look, like a whistler's, like a balloon man's. Though a woman could hold her own, a small fellow lost out, being allowed to display none of his fervor. Even his gore was less grisly—the drillmaster's postmortem took hours and filled up two pails. The smiles were the little man's advocate because they wiped away bravery and pain, both together, and leveled off everything else. This cryptic twitch of the lips at the moment of death began to absorb

Gerry's interest after the rest had become tedium. Most people did wear a smile. Sometimes it wasn't a bit cryptic, it was benevolent, knowing, or blithe and astonished and rather singing. The marks of gritting the mouth through so many weeks of suffering might remain as well, and once in a while somebody's mouth had turned to an unmistakable loathing, but never toward an expression of fright.

Gerry worried because he was able to eat heartily after the sights that he was exposed to and the smells that rose up—powdered bone if he used the saw. Did it mean he would adjust to anything? He got very low-key in mentioning his experiences; he avoided mentioning them. In the barracks at night, the two lines of figures under their blankets unnerved him, with the feet turning up. To lie down himself was like a rehearsal. And the smiles preoccupied him—why in those very last instants? It was a positive action, not merely the mouth going limp as it did in falling asleep. During cancer autopsies, grape-like, gray, horrible bunches were removed, yet the patient smiled. And Babs saw an old army widow die and, practically crying, told how a smile had quietly preempted her face just in the final seconds, after indescribable paroxysms and pain.

The doors to the icebox grew to be like lids on a Pandora's box that he dreaded opening. Then, in a big comedown, the row of bodies inside might look simpleminded when he pulled them out, might look like a row of public wards. A head on its wooden block seemed about to lift and complain. The doctor, to take out the brain, tipped the scalp over the cadaver's eyes like tipping a hat, as though the fellow were mentally dim, which Gerry later tipped back for him.

Colonel Wetthall's duties as court-martial chairman, meanwhile, produced other nasty stories. He seemed to enjoy telling them to Gerry and arguing with him. A prisoner objected during his trial because a guard had woken him capriciously the night before, and he hadn't managed to go back to sleep. He didn't feel he could defend himself alertly.

"It's probably true."

The colonel grinned. "Well, it may well be true that he got woken up, but that isn't something to bring up in front of all of us. He might tell it to the guardhouse sergeant in the morning if he wanted to."

"No, you should be willing to hear him out. He hasn't anyone else."

"He has the guardhouse sergeant. He has the other guards. He has himself. Let me satisfy you, young man," Wetthall said, still friendly, not ungently. "He wasn't beaten. We asked him that. We were laughing just a little, but we asked him. And we asked him whether soldiers ever have to fight without a good night's sleep the night before, but he just whined. He's a whiner."

"He's a prisoner. I think you ought to take the time to hear complaints. That's not going beyond your function, is it? It certainly shouldn't be," Gerry answered, disturbed because the argument tied in with earlier ones.

"If there is any monkey business, sure. If there are violations. This is whining. We told him if he didn't stand up straight we'd strap a board to his back to straighten it. He didn't like that either. He's a deadbeat, really. He stole a camera from a friend of his and now he doesn't want to be confined. And last Sunday his girl friend walked out from the railroad station but the man on duty wouldn't let her in to see him, so he protests to us about that too. It's not something in our discretion."

"He's not a deadbeat, he's a prisoner. He sounds as if he needs a little sympathy."

"Yes, his girl friend does." Wetthall chuckled. "I'm awfully sorry for her. That's a long, hot walk and she does it for this deadbeat. We were tactful, I promise you. We didn't laugh in front of him. We laughed when we went in the other room. I hate to upset you. You have a bleeding heart."

His eyes glittered, sliding away like ball bearings, and the pleasure he appeared to take in teasing Gerry must parallel what he'd felt in the deliberating room. What was he after? How could he relish his power that way and not misuse it? Gerry would be making small talk of the question with the law professors in a few months, but meanwhile the very approach of his independence aggravated his concern.

The barracks commander, Captain Bone, was a shaved-head professional with a brisk, disposable cheeriness, a battlefield, impromptu air. But hard spells succeeded soft no matter who the captain was. They'd sleep on the floor to keep the beds tight for inspection, and polish the floor till it shone like blond hair, rub the brass faucets golden, unscrew the light bulbs to wash them, and seal the gleam on their boots with a lighted match. Like frightened dogs, Fallon and he scrambled under their beds looking for dust, except that they laughed at themselves. Gerry shut himself off in his rooms at the morgue as much as he could. When his time had got whittled down to two months, he was ready to screech from frustration at the previous, squandered twenty-two. The girlfriend illegally brought into the morgue, the diplomacy by which his officers ignored it, bored him, and Babs saw him less anyway, because he didn't use "we" enough, she said, as if his affections weren't permanent.

The occasional weekend in New York City whizzed by. His job had been organized almost to disappearance. The force-fed extravagances of brotherhood that grew up in the barracks were wearying. The sergeants had lost their first novelty. The doctors were knowledgeable only about medicine, although they were so good at dissections that they stirred up his impatience to start on his own career. The colonel remained the best company in spite of the difficulties. A day could pass quickly, working with him, with no hint of their being in the army. But Wetthall withdrew from such familiarity when one of his privates approached discharge, perhaps hurt to see anybody so eager to leave. A new second lieutenant had offended him somehow. During three Draconian days all the property on the books was transferred to him, terrifying the poor man, since it amounted to over a hundred thousand dollars of new responsibility.

Gerry had oiled the tracks for himself, however, until even Captain Bone, whose energy pumped like a piston— who called privates "Duck" from their habit of marching in columns of two—treated him like a short-timer. The bodies departed from his establishment in a wide-stitch, flop-arms fashion, and no one complained. He was popular wherever his errands and other chores took him. Yet he had begun to pick over an uneasy notion, which was to write a letter about the state of affairs regarding Colonel Wetthall. A report would not itself be a court-martial offense, and his discharge was getting too close for most of the standard reprisals. Fallon was working on meningitis at the moment, but by now they were both so well trained that they didn't care.

One Wednesday afternoon the colonel returned from a hearing with his eyes alive and his lips buttoned up. A case of failure to obey. The two of them argued again, the word in this instance being "scum."

"Scum is scum, my friend, I'm afraid," he said, unbuttoning. "We gave him a good chance to think about it. We gave him about six months, as a matter of fact, so we'll see what that does. We may make a new man."

"Oh there's only so much thinking to do, isn't there?" Gerry said ruefully.

"Poppycock. Okay, be anti-authority, fine, while you can. Gather your flowers. Just as long as there's somebody else to get the jobs done and take the heat. A few more years and you'll be having to do it yourself, won't you, or it won't be done? You don't really want eightballs running around loose any more than I do. You'll recognize that. You'll have to face the fact that there is a group of unsavory souls who do best out of circulation. —Sergeant Washburn! Ser-geant Wash-born? I want you!" he called, a hog call, his naturally soft voice cracking.

Gerry was surprised at how decided he felt. A complaint, in theory, should be addressed to the Inspector General, but the I.G. here was just a major, without reputation, besides which he had no wish to blemish the colonel's official record. Treachery enough was involved in any event, because he was still a favorite despite the close scrapes. Maybe all along he'd been treacherous to one person or another in keeping his mouth shut so much. Mad as the idea was, he realized that he was going to go ahead with it and that he wouldn't be thinking it out any further. He could write the Commanding General, not an enemy of Wetthall's, whose action, if any, would be unofficial. Although the general was unlikely to act, after two years here it struck Gerry as appropriate before he left to express, as it were, one suggestion. He delayed a few days and then sat down and drafted carefully.

Commanding General
Headquarters
U.S. Grant Army Medical Center
Firegap, Pennsylvania

3623 Med. Detachment
USGAMC, Firegap, Penn.

17 May 1961

Dear Sir:

I will try to write to you as straightforwardly as I can, not knowing the exact proper form of address, to tell you of something that disturbs me. I have been stationed here, working in the Pathology Section, for twenty months, since completion of training at Fort Sam Houston. It may possibly be that the fact that I will be entering law school in the fall has caused me to take particular notice of the operation of the court-martial and psycho-medical unsuitability Boards. At any rate, I have been very interested and have found I approved of the quality of military justice as I have glimpsed it. Indeed, I am far less critical of the Army as a whole than draftees are generally pictured as being, and, without saying that I am not ready to leave, I have had no meaningful criticisms to make of it as an institution. It is an idealized institution, which can hardly be faulted except where human error comes in. The investigation and trial of court-martial offenses is an example, because, unlike the civilian system by which a man is tried if there are reasonable grounds for suspecting he may have committed a crime, in the Army he will never be brought to trial to begin with unless a comparatively exhaustive investigation has shown it is practically certain that he did commit the crime charged. Much more conclusive proof is expected in the investigative period; and the hearing, as well as an opportunity for him to challenge and counter the evidence, becomes a time when a group of outside officers go over the evidence once again and the process by which it was gathered in a thorough manner. They are administrators and it is a system set up for administrators. The prisoner is innocent until proven guilty, but he is not put on trial until he has virtually been proven guilty, so there is not nearly the need for professional legal men, whom the Army of course could not provide in its countless outposts, as there is in the civilian court system.

I am sorry to be long-winded, but I want to show that my interest has been sincere. The Chief of my Section, Lt. Col. Wetthall, is Chairman of the Court-martial Board at present and also sits on the other Board. I have been working in close, daily contact with him all this while, often with what should only be called friendship, and have been treated fairly by him. What is bothering me is that he seems to have a cruel streak which sometimes affects him very powerfully, a sadistic streak, if you wish—this is difficult to put. Nothing of this has been applied against me, I have only observed it from the sidelines, and he is not responsible for it, it goes without saying. Nor does it affect his excellent medical work. I am trying to say what I have to say without being impertinent or offensive. Since I know that he enjoys friendly relations with you, and seeking also to avoid harmful red tape, I have written to you about it instead of to somebody else. I believe he takes pleasure in the fright and fear of persons under examination, also in sentencing. From his stories, I am certain of this. I have seen and heard it again and again in the past months, and I cannot see how this can help but eventually affect his decisions in such respects as length of sentence or the actual conduct of the hearing itself. I simply would hope that he would not be placed on these Boards anymore, not that his professional duties would be affected in any way. I hope you can see in what limited ways I have been disturbed. Thank you for allowing me to write to you.

> Yours sincerely,
> Gerald Schuyler,
> Pfc., US51462023

Showing the letter to no one, he typed it, held onto it overnight to read again, and delivered it by hand in the course of his rounds the next morning. He hoped that at least the adjutant would be the one to open it first and that the two typist privates at Headquarters Section never saw it at all. He was exhilarated at breakfast, breathing as if he had just won a race. As lengthy as the letter needed to be, coming from him to a general, he had sidestepped saying several things. He had been both clever and honest, he thought, and if any of the general's own observations corresponded to what he had said, it would bring unobtrusive results.

Then he began to go sick. He snuck off to his rooms at the morgue as if he were poisoned, hardly able to breathe, he was so anxious. Now he was caught in the gears. Now he'd be mashed. The letter must have already been opened; he couldn't retrieve it. He stared through the bars on the windows. For his whole life he had been a lucky fool, trusting his luck, proud of his impulsiveness. He thought of the letters to friends, written off the top of his head, which had hurt them. All at once now he would have to pay—in the army, of all insane places. The Commanding General, a man he had never seen and knew nothing about except that the colonel liked him! Brine-green, he leaned on a stretcher and groaned. He wouldn't be called a crackpot and let off. That was only in civil life. You were accountable here—you were run up the flagpole. Oh, good blessed Christ!

In the late afternoon Sgt. Reynolds phoned. "Where you been, Schuyler, sleeping? You're supposed to appear every once in a while, you know. We like your smiles. We like to see you. The colonel wants you."

The colonel, when he knocked and went in, looked almost sicker than he. And Gerry saw instantly that their friendship was ended. As if he were already discharged and home, he realized how fond of the colonel he had been, how much touched by him, with his lonesome "cultural" weekends, his wide open eyes, and mild, inconclusive, highbrowed expression. Once when the corridors had been stacked with flu patients on litters and the civilian workers went off duty at five as though on an ordinary day, the colonel had turned gray and shaky, but not crumpled like this. He looked like he'd gained fifteen pounds in unhealthy places. He gazed in sagging impersonality at Gerry's middle, not telling him to sit down.

"Perhaps we can discuss this letter you've written. Do you have a copy? You kept no copy? Very well, we'll read mine. You're trembling, do you know that? Your hands are trembling. Someday you may look back from a comfortable distance and think you were quixotic in your twenties—you were a half-baked, nice, idealistic young man with a certain amount of guts, and you'll find it an attractive picture, you'll think it was good to be at that age. But I think you'll be wrong. I think you're what you people call a fink. The old-fashioned way to say it is that there are good men and bad men in the world and both of them pretty well stay the way they start out in regard to that feature, whatever else happens to them. So I don't envy you. You have a long life ahead of you, and you may be able to fool yourself or even respect yourself but you won't be able to trust yourself. You've got a little wild man's hell to live in. It will be like having a robber working for you who you can't get rid of. You'll never know what you're going to do next."

They could hear each other breathing. Wetthall looked at the letter, and Gerry trembled from the immense collapse of his fear. He crossed his arms and squeezed his breath in. In his life he had never been so unspeakably sorry. As soon as he'd found out the colonel would be the one to decide what to do with him, he had stopped being afraid!

"We've been glad to have your ideas on the court-martial system. '. . . have found I approved of the quality of military justice as I have glimpsed it. . . . Indeed, I am far less critical of the Army as a whole . . . can hardly be faulted . . .' When is your release date?"

"June thirtieth."

"We won't ask you to start to say sir after all these months. June thirtieth is a fiscal-year release. When would your release be if we decided to keep you on?"

"July eighteenth, sir."

"That sounds like a long wait, doesn't it? We don't want that. As I say, you don't need to sir me. After two years of not saying sir, we don't want to strain you by expecting it now."

Holding his chin in his hands, he was blowing air into his cheeks and pinching it out, not finding it possible to look above Gerry's neck.

"Tell me something. You write here, 'I believe he takes pleasure in the fright and fear of persons under examination, also in sentencing. From his stories, I am certain of this. I have seen and heard it again and again,' et cetera. 'I simply would hope that he would not be placed on these Boards anymore, not that his professional duties would be affected in any way.' You are scrupulous, aren't you? '. . . Thank you for allowing me to write to you.' Has he allowed you to write him?"

"No sir."

"Am I getting pleasure from your fright at this moment?"

"No sir."

"How do I look?"

"You look unhappy, sir. You look upset."

"I guess I look like you look. You look very unhappy, my friend; you look like a sorry specimen. Do you know that, besides the dirtiest, most sudden thing that anyone has ever done to me, this is a punishable offense?"

"I—not at the time, sir. I guess so, sir."

"*Why* is it? No, I take that back, I don't want to bully you. The answer is that this letter should have been shown to me before it was submitted anywhere and then it should have been submitted to Captain Bone, who, if he could not act on it

himself, would have sent it on up to the next man, and so on to
the Commander. But tell me—this is not, I think, an unfair
question—why did you not give it to Captain Bone, because I
think you more or less knew—was it because you didn't want
Captain Bone to know that I have been boasting to my private
soldiers that I was invited to the general's house and his wife's
for tea, and telling my soldiers the outcome of the various cases
I try—only the general himself, instead? Or was it so you
wouldn't get skinned?"

Gerry had a wild blush.

"Why you people don't think anybody but a captain can skin
you I don't know, because they can. You think they're
gentlemen like you in the ranks above captain, don't you? You
think they wouldn't have attained that high rank if they weren't
gentlemen like you."

Humping his chair to face the side wall, he chuckled, clearing
his throat. He looked sideways at Gerry. "I lead an innocuous
life, I assure you. I talk too much. I'm a snob."

Gerry was trying to answer his accusation, but couldn't get
hold of the faintest clue as to what he himself had had in his
mind.

"And you wanted to be dramatic—go straight to the top
rung, right?"

"Yes."

"Why don't you sit down, since we're old friends?"

Gerry mentioned having considered the I.G.

"The I.G. is a kind of a toy. You frighten them if you go to
them." Worn out, he rubbed his eyes. "I think people should
see their letters again. They're not to be sent just fluttering off.
You're a lawyer, and captains are small fry to you. I'll tell you, if
you *were* a lawyer you would be finished after this; you could
start somewhere as an accountant if you were lucky—I'm trembling now. You're not and I am."

He stopped and watched curiously, while Gerry, half blacking out in mortification, tried to cut himself off from the crazy man who had written this ignominious letter.

"Tell me again—here I'm forgetting how bad it is—what did you think the general would do? Could you imagine him doing anything other than sending it down to me?"

"No, I can't. I'm afraid I didn't follow it out."

"Of course that's the easiest, to leave it up to the fates. I'll tell you what's been proven, that I've pampered and shielded a smarty sneak. Has anybody ever surprised you so much?" He laughed, better able to look at Gerry. "Anyhow, to get on with this, you say, 'It may possibly be that the fact that I will be entering law school in the fall . . .' That's just in case he doesn't realize? '. . . the Chief of my Section, Lt. Col. Wetthall . . . What is bothering me is that he seems to have a cruel streak, if you wish—this is difficult to put. . . . he is not responsible for it, it goes without saying. Nor does it affect his excellent medical work.'

"So that's the meat, is it?" he asked after a silence, with a suddenly gay, strong voice. He straightened and pulled his chair up to the table in a soldierly fashion, like a scrappy runt of a field officer with a freckled bald head. "I'm not a man to push to the brink, you know."

"Sir, I can see that I had nothing to go on except guesswork and the way it's put is very very foolish and inexcusable."

"Yes, it's difficult to put. Do you know how you tell a sadist?"

Gerry shook his head.

"A sadist is pretty likely to be the person who talks about sadism a lot and notices it in other people—knows all about who is a sadist and rings the alarm bell, very excited. Or another type is quite different. He's someone who is extremely kind and exceedingly gentle, who can almost, you might say, be counted upon to do the kindest thing when he is in a position of power and when it actually comes down to the point of doing any-thing. This might not remain the case forever, but if you supposed that I was a sadist, for instance, and from knowing me well, as you say, you knew I would probably be leaving the army within a couple of years and that these board duties rotate, besides, and any and all decisions are passed up to the Com-mander for confirmation"—he took a deep, jerky breath and slapped the letter—"you might get an A, my friend, if you concluded that the sentences for these couple of years were going to remain just as lenient as the Commander was going to allow.

He waited.

"Nothing to say? Young man, I want you to keep out of my vicinity as much as you can between now and the end of the fiscal year. I've told you how I don't envy you. I'm going to tell Reynolds to give you more work than you've had, because you've gotten away with murder in the past year. And I want to hear one thing more, if it's not tormenting you. Why is it that I'm not charging you? Do you think this letter won't be talked about because I'm not? Or am I afraid you'll think you were right and that I'm a sadist if I do?"

"Sir, I'm sorry, I'm very—"

"Get out of here, you're dirt to me," he said, in the grand, army style.

The purged self-possession the colonel finished with lasted for several days before his muddy qualities caught up with him again, although he didn't single people out as much. Gerry went around with runny bowels and dizzy spells, digesting the scene. At moments he still believed he'd done the decent thing; the alteration in the colonel seemed to prove it. He thought he'd stuck his neck out when most people would not have cared. Besides, it might have been the adjutant who'd read the letter, not the general, which would provide another reason for

Wetthall to drop the matter. When reviewed, the incidents that had aroused him continued to, but he realized the colonel hadn't wanted to crush him despite feeling betrayed and that he had oversimplified and been too swift and cavalier about risking someone's career. The memory stung. Sometimes he thought the colonel's predictions were true, because he could relate a bunch of half-cocked blunders of his that went way back and could conjure up a future of ever savager impulses and narrower escapes.

In June he grew almost teary; whole weeks were bathed in nostalgia, a process he had watched as other people's discharges approached. Now it was his turn and, though he hardly spoke with the new transferees, with anybody else who had been around for more than six months, he stopped along the corridors and talked, leaning an elbow on the wall. His days were spent in being congratulated, being asked how he was feeling. As if pregnant, he shared the news. He grinned down gently at his "whites," like an ethnologist, and tolerantly stood reveille, his sleeping limbs slumped into the regulation posture. When he attended Troop Information lectures, he'd known two officers before the present one and his impatience was gangrenous. He was as tender toward himself as a man healing after injuries, unwinding the bandages and wondering that he has survived.

To ceremonialize the two-week mark, he and Fallon and Pvt. Babs held a candlelight party in the morgue. They decided that they couldn't invite newcomers, finally, and sat with wine and pastries as a party of three. The candles were fun, the grinning was fun, although there wasn't a great deal to say. Fallon was a four-square type, domesticating the table with his elbows until it became a comfortable size, with that heaviness Gerry had gotten fond of. Babs, urchin-like and unyielding as ever, had never accepted either his view of her or of himself, so he was glad they were free of each other. But he was worried because she had no prospects, no one to help her. He was afraid that, a month or so after he left, she would panic at the civilian plans she had made and reenlist in the army instead. She peppered out tight little jokes about the world outside, and Fallon told how the baseballs rained down in July in Claremont Park, so that you gripped your head. Gerry didn't say much, conscious of the flashier program which awaited him.

The candles shone through Bab's hands, when she cupped them, with an astonishing pink iridescence. Even Gerry and Fallon could watch their blood move. Fallon said he remembered reading that a candle wouldn't shine through a dead man's hand. He suggested they try out the rule. Gerry didn't like the idea especially, because he'd become still brisker with the bodies since having been told by the colonel that he had a sadistic side too. With the candles glowing before them, however, and not many subjects to talk about, they went in to test if the story were true on a middle-aged corporal from one of the anti-aircraft sites who had been autopsied during the afternoon. He had died in the hospital's mental wing, the cause of his death, a brain tumor, not having been diagnosed properly. It wouldn't have been operable, but the doctors had had a sad time, regretting not letting his family visit him and not having fixed him in quiet surroundings.

Looking down at the man's face again, holding the hot, dripping candle, Gerry immediately recognized the wrongness of what they were up to. Nobody was eager to unfold the hands—his slowness slowed them all down. The aberrant behavior that had confused the doctors hadn't left any tokens behind. In a relaxed way the corporal seemed more soldierly than a middle-aged corporal might usually look, and, if he wasn't too bright, he looked steady. One nostril had widened slightly, as if he were just going to smile a little on that side of his mouth, as if he were with a friend, having finished a hard, marching day, and, pleasurably enough, was just a bit bored. The business was terribly awkward. They were fumbling at it when two starchy MPs, along with the AOD and the MOD and the NCOD, unlocked the door to bring in another body. This interruption seemed to fit in with the silliness of the project so well that for a minute they didn't realize they were in trouble.

The Medical Officer of the Day was an intern who had watched the postmortem, and he glanced at Gerry and at the dead corporal with disapproval, nodding goodbye to his colleague, who would take charge. The Administrative Officer, by mischance, was the provost marshal, a most effective major who lived off-post with his family and who wore an insignia mustache.

"Who are you?"

"Sir, I work here. I'm in the Pathology Department," Gerry said.

"Where are your clothes? You're not in uniform."

"I'm off duty, sir."

The major grimaced at what was in front of him, growing leery and clipped. "What is this nonsense? Why are you here then? What are you trying to burn, for heaven's sake?" He walked quickly through the other three rooms and back.

"Sir, it looks strange, but it really was nothing particular," Gerry said, following him at a distance. "We were trying out an old wives' tale."

"You were having a party, I gather. Whose glasses?"

"We'd heard—we were wondering whether it's true—that a candle doesn't shine the same way through a dead man's hand. I'm sorry. It sounds crazy, I know. We were shining it through," explained Gerry numbly.

"Yes, if you work here you know it's off-limits better than anyone else."

Fallon blew out the candle and Gerry helped stow the new arrival onto an icebox tray. The NCOD was the assistant supply sergeant who gave them their clean sheets every week, but he was braced as impersonally as the MPs for the obvious court-martial, as if to witness a ritual ordeal.

"It's pretty cut-and-dried, isn't it?" said the major. He wrote down the time and their names. He sighed, looking around. "See if Captain Bone is still on post, will you, Ashlen? I'm going to get your captain in. We might as well. If you like to burn bodies, you can look at this one. He was a real smart guy. He hasn't a flashlight and he wants to see if his gas tank is empty, so he looks down the hole with a match."

"We weren't trying to burn anything, sir," Fallon told him. Gerry explained again that they were testing an old rule of thumb.

The captain came, with his commission riding lightly on his shoulders, a more adjustable type altogether, but he too screwed up his face at the mess they had gotten themselves into, in their lounging sweaters and all.

"That's sheer absolute idiocy. Who was the bright one? Who had the brainstorm? Can't let anybody off?" He had Babs in mind, but before they could agree, he said, "No, we can't. It's a restricted area. She's not a baby."

Wetthall was called because of his prickly reputation where his own section was involved, and he turned up, although they had hoped that he wouldn't. He listened to the accounts, regarding Gerry with flat dislike and the others assembled with some distaste.

"Don't you realize these people when they're about to get out of the army think that they own the place? It's a wonder they don't run many more tests!" He laughed. After first clasping his hands behind him as if he were hearing an irksome speech, when that wasn't comfortable he stuck them into his pockets instead, and then finally crossed his arms on his chest. He showed none of the ritual air of the NCOs or the duty officer, never mentioned proceedings being taken, and, when the major did, opened his eyes in surprise and averted them as if the notion were news indeed. Gerry, appalled, fighting the sensation off, all at once felt completely saved.

"It doesn't quite have the smell of a court-martial situation, Major, would you say? When you compare it with some of the other things, it seems short of the borderline." He gave a mansion-porch smile, seeing company off.

Captain Bone stood very straight with his eyebrows raised, so that one's heart couldn't help but go out to him; but the provost marshal was a tougher cookie, who also knew how to spread on a smile.

"It seems to be clear as a clam to me. You've got it down like a laundry list. You've got the candle, no less, whatever exactly that means. You've got the wine. You've got the girl in on it. You've got the poor corpse inside there. Whether you add them up upside down or right side up it's still awful funny." He did a palms up. "I'm responsible, Colonel, and it may look sort of like a bad joke to you and to me, but if the relatives knew they wouldn't feel the same way."

"If the relatives knew there had been an autopsy or if the relatives knew the results of the autopsy, they wouldn't be pleased. It's a wretched little piece of history," Wetthall remarked, touching his gaze along the shelves of specimen jars. In subdued ridicule he turned from there to the crease in the major's sleeves and the militant line of his shirt front and fly.

"Well, with all due respect to you, this is my night, sir, I'm afraid. I'm responsible. It seems to be very much cut-and-dried," said Major Kinsey.

"If we had a martinet working in here he'd probably be buggering the corpses," the colonel said softly in his cracked voice. "This is part of my lab. I know the personnel who are concerned. They say they were shining a candle through a dead man's hand, which is an extraordinarily stupid thing to have been doing, almost beyond belief, and you might have to admit that they're missing a screw, but it doesn't impress me as suitable for court-martial action. If Captain Bone chooses to give punishment on the company level, that might be appropriate, but a court-martial action would not be. We can discuss it tomorrow morning with the general if you'd like."

He put on a cordial smile. He excused the enlisted men. The major walked away angry, looking more like a colonel than he. Captain Bone went out to his car, amused, maybe vaguely disgusted. Wetthall left for the officers' billiards room at such a speed Gerry couldn't keep up with him, which was all he was trying to do, just stay behind him.

KWAN'S CONEY ISLAND

THERE WAS A SAINT IN THE STREETS, a bland silver man about one-fourth-sized who was rolling along on a rubber-wheeled cart while a priest in lace walked in front reading the blessing. Two lines of men gently pulled the lead ropes and behind the saint's cart a large number of women in black carried candles. A uniformed band of fifteen played a salute to anybody who came up with a dollar bill to be pinned to the saint's vestments. "Wait a minute! Wait a minute. Not so fast," said a butcher coming out of his store after the crowd had gone by. He wore a black band on his arm and, holding his dollar, he kept at a sensible step to catch up with them. The band turned, like everyone else, to wait and, when he'd delivered it, did the salute, all the cheeks puffed, the instruments facing him. He got a saint's card from the priest, which his wife kissed.

Kwan nodded familiarly to the marchers. These parades happened almost every month. He followed until the fireworks stage, when a string of firecrackers were laid down for a block and the head man waved his breast-pocket handkerchief a long time, swearing because his assistants at the opposite end couldn't figure out what he meant. Then a shocking great war cannonade went off, filling the air with its smell and smoke. The kids ran the length of the fuse just ahead of the blasts, and yellow and blue and red stains were left in the street which would last till the next occasion. The saint was rolled into a storefront to stay.

Kwan had been downtown for Saturday night and had come back late on the bus. This morning, delightfully logy, he'd lain in bed past eleven o'clock, although he was never a sound sleeper. He lived in the back of his laundry, not to save money so much as because he had gotten to be rather crusty and could do without constant company. He liked company only in short doses. After a get-together he took at least a couple of days to digest whatever he'd heard and several more days to finish enjoying it. He had lived in Pittsburgh for many years, so to live here in New York a few dozen blocks from the central neighborhood of his own people was a luxury. In his block were black men and Puerto Ricans and Sons of Adam, as he called the Hasidic Jews, and Italians, as he called the Germans, Poles, Greeks, and Italians, and miscellaneous bums and bearded young scholars. He had a Russian church and a Spanish church alongside his business and, all in all, he could pass in and out with a fine anonymity. Sundays in August now he went to the beach, thinking over the gossip of Saturday night and the fixes his friends had gotten themselves into. Even on a cool day he would go because of the sweltering week he'd put in, as well as the sweltering week to come. He was middle-aged, dressed in his next-to-best suit and a clovered sport shirt, with the mild roundish face of a member of the amphibian family, except for his humorous mouth and firm chin.

The hydrants were going but nobody soaked him as he went past; the Puerto Ricans were after their own. It was a day in the eighties with a marvelous high sky the blue of an organdy robe. He took the subway, reading a Chinese newspaper until the tracks emerged above ground. Having chosen his seat especially, he sat back, his hands clasped in his lap, blinking in the sun, and fanned by a dry city breeze. Although his appearance was staid, he was just as pleased at the holiday as the children who chased back and forth in the car. They were more than pleased—they jumped on the seats, they shoved each other against other passengers and part way out of the window. The train made a great many lackadaisical stops, while Kwan mused down at the street below. At Coney Island the pour of humankind off the platform and the festival babble and crush got him energetic.

There were mynah birds telling fortunes, merry-go-rounds making music, coin-slotted player pianos. On the hurtling rollercoaster, people screamed and screamed. From the pots at Korn's Korn came a scarifying smell like flesh burning, and the teenagers, running in front of the traffic, plunged for the beach. It was all too much, of course, and reminded him of scenes from his boyhood in China, but he was detached and quick on his feet, inconspicuous, knew what he liked, and liked this contrast with the rest of the week.

He went to his bathhouse establishment. STEAM, the signs said. A lot of the men spent the whole day reading the newspaper in their cubicles. They sunned for a bit on the roof, steamed in the steam room, and never went out on the beach. Kwan sampled the services, getting his money's worth. The fat stomachs on the Italians amused him. Though he was certainly no muscle-man, they were so laughably fat that as soon as they took off their belts they had to hold onto their bellies. Their testicles bulged like bunches of onions. To squeeze in for a shower was like having to push through a herd of beach balls. It was always quarrelsome, because most of them weren't alone through the week like he was but were standing up for their rights in some busy business establishment, and they couldn't lay off on Sunday. And the black-white business was tense. Only a handful of blacks came in to change, but today one of them attached on to Kwan to try to get into the showers. He was in the next cubicle and he offered Kwan part of a sandwich, struck up a conversation until Kwan left with his towel, and then hurried to swallow and stand up too, more and more nervous about it.

"It's pretty packed, huh?"

"Plenty room," Kwan assured him.

The trouble was that his fear was contagious; for a moment Kwan was afraid to go into that bald gleaming mass of bodies himself, forgetting that nobody ever objected to him. The black man hardly looked at him, he was so busy being nonchalant and looking ahead to the white men's faces.

"Any space?"

Kwan paused beside the Negro, but there were so many people talking that nobody answered. He pushed through to find a spot, the man tagging after, putting a shoulder in Kwan's stream of water and sloshing his front with one hand. It was a crazy room, with shapes such as you never saw on the street, and much genital-fussing and belly-rubbing.

The exit to the beach went under the boardwalk, where the whites were the jittery ones. The shade was dazzlingly striped with thin lines of sun and a good crowd of people had sprawled in the cool twilit sand. Mothers held kids. The passive families with their spraddled-out postures and scraps of food reminded Kwan of a refugee crowd, and the stripes across everything were doubly weird, but the sea glittered peacefully blue. He had on a new bathing suit and his toes had not grown as old or as crooked as some of these fellows' toes. Adding it up, he cut not a bad figure, he thought. Nobody took exception to him.

A bunch of colored children tore by, throwing handfuls of sand. There were drunks with beer cans, tough policemen, and propped, melancholy souls alone on the part of the beach where everyone else was in transit. They lay on one elbow with their lonely detective novel and their plaid thermos bottle and their brown fleabag blanket from home. It was stop-go. A pair of whites would find themselves on a collision course with three blacks and suddenly stop. By the water the hot sand got cold. Jammed family groups whooped it up; screwballs were yelling. The continual verging on violence was tiresome but didn't directly affect Kwan, who picked his way out beside one of the breakwaters until his body was lapped by the waves. Facing the sun, he braced his back against a large rock and dug his heels in, loving the suctioning. This was his favorite time of the week, right now. He wiggled around for the perfect position, worried that soon the day would be gone, that he wasn't happy enough, but he was. The light, multiplied on the water, was a week's worth of sun. He had seaweed to scrub with and salt on his lips. He smiled so much that he wasn't aware he was smiling, and was all the time closing his eyes to enjoy them closed and then opening them to watch the shimmer and action. Probably five thousand kids were being taught how to swim just in the area in front of him, which made for a steady myriad blare, the yeows and shrieks yiping out of it. Jumping, jumping, jumping, jumping—there was scarcely space for the waves to roll in. When the wind cut the hooting, it blew back again. Old-man-in-the-moon faces bobbed up to blow out the water and suck in some air. Horses chased horses. Mothers were teaching by every method, including the drown-'em-and-laugh-at-'em-cry, if only because they themselves were scared. The lifeguards paddled on little rafts which the fishy kids tried to catch up with, and once they had a shark scare, when the police helicopter started to swoop. A guy clambered out covered with black steamship oil, having swum through a slick. He'd been the shark. In the distance the regular skyride screams were like crying dolls squeezed.

Five children crept past after crabs, although the rocks had been hunted clean. Kwan tried to converse with them with avuncular dignity, pretending to peer round his feet in case a crab might be hiding there. He liked their shouts and the teeming water and teeming beach, the women in bouncing bathing suits. While he regretted not having had children, this was not a gnawing or painful feeling because it had never seemed possible. Marriage had never been much of a hope. He'd paid court to several ladies but always as one of so many suitors that the family and daughter had toyed with him, letting him know how privileged he was. Even so, he had various dear memories of the onanist's kind—vigils outdoors, or missing a meal to send flowers he knew that the girl would ignore.

Sometimes he'd encountered a colored woman who would come in the back and allow him to tickle her a little instead of charging her for her laundry, and then he had hoped that a permanent amicability might grow up between them. But each time afterwards when he mulled it over, he realized it would only amount to a lot of tickling—no work. If he wanted to share his life with someone, he needed a helper. The flight to Hong Kong to bring back a wife required an enormous sum. To be sure, he had saved toward it, but he was an occasional gambler and he loved his other few pleasures too much.

The mobs were a piece of his childhood, the kids smeared with black sand. He strolled way down to the fishing pier and sat against a green piling. He saw an eel caught and a beer-bottle fight between the men on the pier and the men in the motor boats which were putting about, tangling some of the lines. There was a fight on the beach as well. The white lifeguards in the towers close by had to jump down and help one of their bunch against ten or twelve Puerto Ricans. The police got into it with roaring and clubs and the kids on the sidelines grabbed several girls by the heels and dragged them around, scaring them into hysterics. It was serious for an instant; then it fragmented. The unearthly hordes of people, picnicking, petting, quietly wading, swallowed everything up.

With sharp interest, Kwan watched the ocean-going ships rendezvous with the pilot boat at the mouth of the Narrows. As a boy he had wanted to go to sea and still thought of himself as half seaman, especially because of his one long sea journey. At night in his shop he listened for toots from the harbor, sniffing the salt smells. He liked to walk, so he walked some more, keeping a count of the ships he saw and prolonging the afternoon's activity. When people spat near his feet on the sand he spat back, if not near enough to set off a brawl. The beach was extremely hot. He got up on his toes and trotted under the boardwalk again with the shade-loving crew. The Seashell Bar was there, a whole line of bars, and this was his day for American food. He leaned on the counter as sauerkraut was forked onto his sausage—"Very good stuff. More, man." With big mouthfuls he ate a whole lot. A raving white man kept pulling his trousers off, while the cops attempted to tie them on during the wait for the ambulance. Finally they needed to handcuff him in order to keep them on. He shrieked like a factory whistle and collected a crowd. Kwan scraped with his teeth at a candied apple and winced at the smell of the cooking corn.

The sea was a sizzling, glistening blue. He watched the Parachute Jump, the kids doing stunts. He watched the Diving Bell sink down in its tank where it was nosed by the Porpoise Herd. Couples being jolted out of the funhouse doors at the end of their ride were bloated by mirrors to squeal a last squeal. At the Torture House an elephant was mashing a canvas man underfoot. Santa Claus laughs came up from him. The sign "Chinese Water Torture" intrigued Kwan, since he couldn't guess what that might be. Finally he paid the twenty-five cents. The House was a tent behind a board facade, and the Water Torture was not featured prominently. Both victim and tormentor were yellow as bile, the latter chuckling, apparently. The victim looked up with the face of a calf about to feed, head twisted around to catch hold of the teat. He was papier mâché, and a make-believe faucet dripped on him. Quite accurate characters in a pencilled balloon said, "Let me go." Kwan grinned at all this, but some of the other exhibits made him squint; he had squint lines engraved almost like a sun-squint.

There was a live show. A fat man climbed slowly onto the stage. "Folks can come right down close to me where you can see everything and hear everything. No need to be afraid of me . . . ." His face was tattooed as if he'd wished to obliterate it, not simply to become a rarer freak. He had a display case of hatpins and needles and two rows of drinking glasses.

"All you good people want to see everything, want to hear everything. That's what you have here, all the odd people," he said, filling the glasses to different levels, and continued in a mesmerizing, biting voice, "My name is Musical Tons." He laughed to get his body shaking, groaning at the discomfort. "I'm fat, but since I'm not as fat as some I'm also musical." He licked his finger and began to rub the glasses' rims. He did "Dixie" and "I Could Have Danced All Night." But the audience grew sarcastic and whistled along. "Mary, to my right, is one of our features. She's going to talk to you about herself in her own words and will be glad to answer any of your questions. Please listen carefully."

"Now you were told outside on the paper that I would show you underneath my dress, and that's what you are seeing," said Mary, who was unbuttoning her dress in mannish haste. The people giggled with whispers. Faint howls drifted from the rollercoaster. She wore a bathing suit. "I am a Christian woman and I do not show you underneath my bathing suit. It is the same. The ladies may feel of anywhere they wish to be convinced that it is real. The gentlemen may feel of anywhere where they would feel their sisters or their mothers. Now I have cards for ten cents which show myself and I will write on them my name Mary in my own handwriting, which is very good."

She spoke fast and she wrapped the dress around her like a towel.

"Now I am called the Crocodile Woman, which is because my skin is like the thick skin or the hide of a crocodile. It is because of a disease, and which is not infectious, do not worry. I am a Christian woman the same as your wife or your mother. Now I have a message for you, which is that God loves you. Enjoy the life which God has given to you, enjoy your skin, be thankful."

"Thank you, Mary," Musical Tons said into the microphone. "May I direct our friends back to myself? I am going to perform what has been called in the newsprint a remarkable demonstration of hardihood. Pay close attention, if you please."

He took his shirt off. There were hooks through his nipples, and he picked up two five-pound weights from the floor with them. "I'd do the heavier ones if we had a bigger crowd." He smiled around. He had separate smiles for the whites and the blacks but in both cases bitter with scorn. As he swung into doing his stuff, what politeness he'd had before peeled away; he was intense.

"What I do mostly is stick these pins through myself. Want me to?"

"Yeah," called the crowd, caustic and mostly young. He grinned at them and they back at him. The Santa Claus *ho's* came from the man being mashed by the elephant outside, and Kwan's squint was well-rooted by now, not much more distressed than a standard sun-squint but limiting the amount that the eyes took in.

"You do?" Turning a bit toward the knot of whites, he dawdled, as if such a personal stunt was humiliating to perform in front of a bunch of Negroes, who were quick to sense this, however. Several pressed in, looking at all those blue bruises.

"Which arm?" he asked.

"Left!" they shouted. And plenty of whites were panting as well, until his contempt grew so delicious to him he couldn't bear it and wheeled around to the blacks again.

"How about both arms?"

People broke into smiles and nodded. He leaned from the stage, stroking the longest hatpins. "You may expect I sterilize these things. No, as a matter of fact, just the opposite." He dropped them and rolled them under his shoe. "The trouble is, a platform like this is never awfully dirty; not the real vicious germs. How about it? Put some on for me, would you? Give me some germs."

Ha! They were startled. Those who didn't freeze up were excited. "You want to get poorly, huh? Over here, babe!"

Musical Tons mixed his colors and took from the young and the old, leaning out to give everybody a chance to contribute the smudge off their hands. The women acted as if they were touching a snake, and one fellow had a real brainstorm and licked the pin when it came to him.

"Good. Let's get the worst of it. Give me some more."

He picked a white volunteer to help push the needles through. "You're not much use, are you? Is he, folks?" It was hard going with the first one, particularly on the far side of his arm. The point was dulled so that nothing important inside would be cut. Once the pain started, though, his zest went away; he was deadpan. It seemed like distasteful labor to him rather than pain. Kwan felt twinges penetrating his limbs too.

Anguished figures around the room were painted with blood, but he might have been digging a sewer hole. When he had hatpins sticking through both his arms, "How's this?" he said. "Enough, or do you want 'em through my legs too?"

"Up your old ass, man. Let's see the whole thing!"

"He smiled toothily like a dog." Everywhere? Okay, but your job's the filth. I want all you have. Armpits, that's right, you got the idea."

The racial divisions were gone. It was between those who froze and those who warmed. The pins that were already in obstructed his muscles when he was pushing the new pins through and he looked like a man from Mars equipped for space signals. "How about it?" He pointed to marks on the side of his neck. "Sometimes if I have a big crowd I'll put one through here. Are you people big?"

"Yeah, big. Big as butter," they yelled, with the grins of a gangster movie emptying.

He laughed. "No, you're not. You're too small." He drew out the pins and rubbed the blood drops at each exit point into one of his hands like a powder.

Kwan loafed in a bingo parlor for an hour—a collection of souls who were more his own age. The sun got low. The whistle-pitched roar from the beach subsided. Instead there were drumming parties and bonfires, shouting and stone-throwing. A girl belly-danced. Gangs of kids with handkerchiefs around their heads were swinging clubs. The beach was like a checkerboard, with whites in certain parts and blacks in other parts. Kwan watched the pitching machines pitch baseballs and watched the Scorpion, the Steeplechase. The lights strung over all of the rides went on, and a boy ran along the boardwalk setting the wastebaskets afire. Kwan steamed in his bathhouse again. He sat in a bar, played bingo another half-hour, then saw the jail pen cleared. As this was underneath the boardwalk, an amphitheater was formed around it by the ramps going up. A large crowd gathered, and, since the prisoners came out singly to the paddy wagon, the process was a long one, each fellow making his moment in the limelight just as dramatic as he could. For some it was the last steps of a death march, for some the last steps to the stake. They stalked like concentration camp victims. They wept dementedly and stumbled, protesting, with glances at the sky. Soon afterward the riot that had been brewing finally broke out. It wasn't anything to see, just cobra-mongoose-jumping and strangled yells, figures running dimly and hammering down with their sticks. First the Italians were outnumbered, and then the blacks. New blacks came, more Italians, and then again new blacks, who were sweeping the bench when the cops sirened in.

Kwan wandered through a side alley to get a last feel of the sand. He took his shoes off for the fifth time that day. He couldn't decide whether to go straight home or stop downtown along the way.

He noticed a colored woman who was sitting against a post in the darkness near him. "Hey you," she said. He was cautious—he had started to leave—but turned and edged toward her, kicking ice cream cups and paper plates.

"I'm Chinese," he said.

"I know you're Chinese. Nobody's mad at you. Nobody's going to beat you up." She laughed. The feet on the boardwalk sounded over them.

Lying down, he put his hands behind his head and clasped the post. She fixed a piece of cardboard in the position of a lean-to. Although she was only a youngster, she had a face with glamorous, rich lines, a nose that flared out when she smiled, and very pretty creases in her forehead with which she could pretend surprise.

"I'm Crystal."

He was impatient now. In his old boardinghouse a Cuban girl had tapped along the rows of single rooms each night, being quick and businesslike.

But she insisted. "Say it."

"Clystal."

"Crystal!" she giggled. "No, Crystal. Say it."

"Clystal." He clutched the pole and watched her tongue.

"Crystal. You trying?"

"I hold on," Kwan said.

"Yes, you hold on as hard as you can. First say it, though."

"Clystal."

"Crystal!" she shrieked in giggles, making him wait.

A FABLE OF MAMMAS

THERE ONCE WAS A POWERFUL KING who became very harsh to the Loylars who lived in his country, a people looked at in somewhat the same light as Gypsies, although they lived peaceably enough, being farmers and herders. They were not quite regarded as having the national blood in their veins. "Oilies" they were called. The state granaries and shops were not open to them. They must find a non-Loylar to buy their food and resell it to them or to dispose of their crops. Non-Loylar teachers and medical men couldn't minister to them, but no Loylar was allowed to attend a professional school. A Loylar must take off his hat to a full citizen in the street and bow. Yet instead of opening the borders so that they could make their escape to the Balkans where they were said to originate from, King Igor shut down the borders completely so none could leave, as if he thought they existed as subjects of his only for him to tyrannize over.

Igor II was a military man in ideal more than in practice. He liked to sit down to his lunch on time and hurried indoors whenever it rained. Realizing this, as a man of humility, he respected his soldiers all the more. He wanted a disciplined, well-generaled nation, everything in its order, someone at the bottom and somebody on top, and in regard to the Loylars, an entire mercantile class had grown up which factored for them in all of their business. Igor was an unsure man who believed it was better to make no change than to fuddle in haste with established customs arrived at, not by any one person's judgment, but by the nation's unfolding wisdom. So he pursed up his mouth in dismay if he heard of a riot occurring and faithfully read through the protest petitions which arrived at the court afterwards from the Loylars, even though it was never his policy to grant a request which was couched urgently, only later when everybody had forgotten the plea except for the King. He kept lots of advisers around but was swayed by each of them to distrust the rest, since when he'd ask what one fellow thought of another, he was likely to get an equivocal smile which seemed to say, "Well, Your Grace is a generous man, and *he* knows where his bread is buttered." Igor seldom dismissed a favorite, preferring to keep him hanging about the anterooms uneasily, where Igor could nod and smile at him while hurrying past in the midst of his present circle of councillors. His theory was that these ex-intimates made up a sort of a watchdog committee. The King had a vulnerable narrow nose, a thin voice, a head going bald but refined in shape. His expressions wished to appear agreeable but could readily change to peevishness. The palace had gotten full of people whom he skipped by, smiling sociably, although when he trusted somebody he would walk up to the man with a certain bluntness.

Janice, the Queen, was a conscientious, long-headed person. Her lineage was very old, and she was forgiving if humorless in directing the household. She had one baby son whom she adored, grateful to have had him at all at her age, and whom she intended to raise as a self-abnegating sovereign. Until his incredible disappearance, she kept herself well-occupied and in hand. She liked flowers and singing gardeners and carp in the fountains. She liked people who were removed from herself— match girls, milkmaids, gnarled sturgeon fishermen. She was a womanly woman under her crown, though her womanliness didn't do very much for her. Her hair, finely done, was not thick at the roots, the way the King would have enjoyed. Her forearms were skinny. And because her carriage drives in the afternoon went west, south, east, and then north from the palace in rotation, every fourth drive brought her smack up against the edge of a large Loylar district, with its street smells of sewage and picked-over garbage, its ragged washlines, and forlorn, sickly children. The neighborhood crowds, a bit giddy with misery and nutritional deficiencies, fell silent and sullen. Her escort of Houseguard Cavalry clattered close in a diamond formation about her, while the sun glinted on them. She detested the mustachioed soldiers at that moment. There were a few haunting cries from the children playing in the gutter naked or playing on a bone pile. A peddler held up a pulpy orange as if to present it to her, but she couldn't tell whether he did this in insolence, because all the fruit on his cart was as spoiled. Appalled by the pitiful scenes and the smells, she nevertheless refused to let her staff alter the route. If it was there to be seen, the Queen ought to see it. Her husband agreed with her that a backward people like the Loylars should not be encouraged to move to the capital, where their old way of life was impossible. Without sunlight and streams running by and the regulation of the work of each season, their customs dissolved, their homes became dungheaps, and they took to the bottle.

Indeed, a revival of serfdom was being spoken of, only held off by the King's suspicions and indecision—he didn't want to go overboard. His Chief of Staff had suggested the measure precisely for its humanizing effect. A soldier's soldier, he was a grizzled ascetic whose command regiment traveled as swiftly as any in Europe, ready to feint an attack at the drop of a hat. He was impatient with the temporizing of various courtiers. Soldiers knew the shortness of life, and that a life was a life, that a man might lose his life to any man and no dishonor in it, that a man was only as strong as his arms and legs. The Loylars as serfs would not go hungry because, like troops on maneuvers, they would be fed before anyone else; and they would be asked to do nothing their taskmasters weren't willing to do right alongside. Didn't his own troopers grin when he appeared at their head for a cross-country run?

"The General is like the duck which thinks that all birds can swim," the Chief Councillor said. "Every landlord turns into a sergeant at heart?" His opinion was that freedom of movement must be preserved, serfdom being subtly insidious for all concerned. He was a glamorous, sleep-skipping, but paunchy man of forty-eight, an ironist, a misanthrope, and yet ambitious for his country. Twenty-seven years ago he had come into prominence because he had saved a rib of Igor's great-grandfather, when the grave and the royal cathedral enclosing it were sacked by invaders. He had come forward with memorably cheerful *sang-froid*, in the midst of a wailing peasantry and the routed, disorderly army, to the King, Igor's father, whom he had never seen before, and said, "I have saved a bone!"

Miscegenation with the Loylars was outlawed, meanwhile, and since it was believed that they shouldn't own land, their land was seized and leased back to them. The middlemen who handled their transactions combined in a guild and raised the fees charged. With shuttered windows, the wretched Oilies stayed out of sight when they could, or else went into the woods to obscure huts and caves, living on hedgehogs, turtles, and greens of the field, so that the townspeople said they were thieves. Their houses were searched, their families were cuffed, and feeling against them only increased. Several young bloods were killed trying to cross the border, and delegations waited upon the King. Finally, however, a lassitude seemed to settle over a great many of them. They lay low, living off what they raised in their yards, if they could. The various traders who dealt with them chuckled and said they were busy making babies again and that there was an art to managing them.

Then the young prince, a boy of four, disappeared. It was thought that some hardened kidnapper had him. The police and the King, while they searched systematically, waited for a huge ransom demand. Weeks went by. Criminal haunts were turned upside down. The command regiment quick-marched between market towns. The Queen and Queen Mother pled publicly for his release. A description was posted and cried everywhere: a blond-faced boy, from the Queen's Scandinavian ancestry. There weren't many details to give for a boy so young, and not all of them suitable—his mother had called him Meadowmouse in the first months of his life.

The corps of courtiers got an overdue purge. The playroom staff, questioned nearly to death, could volunteer nothing beyond the fact that since it had been a warm autumn day, the French doors onto the lawn were opened. The Chief Councillor feared that the King of Wallenda, neighboring on the south, might have stolen the child as a bargaining pawn, except nothing was heard from that quarter either. Why would a prince be kidnapped and notice not be immediately given? The King was quite popular and no one supposed the diffident Loylars might be involved in such an audacious exploit. After the first seizures of their land, they had stopped rioting; they'd simply looked startled. Even in good times they didn't club together, being a "mountaintop people," as the phrase went—sandy-haired, light-eyed, with agile bodies. They wore goat-hair sweaters and whistled communications to each other across the gulches. They cut pipes to smoke and cut flutes to blow and some of them spoke a subdialect that only a few persevering priests comprehended.

The idea took root that the boy must have wandered outside by himself—proud Igor inclining to this when he heard it. As numbers of beggar children were always about, somebody, noticing such a brave toddler, doubtless had carried him home to adopt. Advertisements of this possibility were put out. He could hang from his father's outstretched hand like a hussar; and his parents, more frankly, let it be known that he pronounced "horse" as "loss" and that he confused "barber" for "soldier," though in general he was ahead of his age at learning to talk.

None of these measures produced the child, however. Each day was a spoonful of lye in the stomach. Oh, plenty of women pushed up to the Servers' Gate with orphans they'd snatched off the street (not always orphans). Like the mothers of children who act on the stage, they exhorted the sentries to bring them before the King right away. And the street children spent a delirious month being primped, fed, and traipsed to the palace, dressed in new clothes, which afterwards they ran away in. The girls clipped their hair to get in on it, and they all caught on to say "barber" and "loss." As a whole, the nation felt baffled and ashamed, as after a regicide. The Queen was sent by her doctors to the June Castle, while the anxious King, fierce and forbearing by turns, shuttled about. He had cooled toward his closest advisers. What had seemed like dispassionate statesmanship in the Councillor, for example, struck him as indifference now. He was too supple, too *amused* a man. And the General, for all the huzzas he drew from the troops of the line, was childless himself and, besides, had seen too many youngsters die. His Majesty was usually absent from the Commonpleas Audience, but when he showed up he behaved unpredictably, granting reprieves, accepting alibis, or else turning suddenly merciless.

The stage mothers left off at last; the urchins slept in the alleys in peace. Despairing, the Queen prayed obsessively in her chapel, believing that only long years of prayer had conquered her previous infertility.

Events stood thus when a Loylar woman arrived one day at the Palace Mall. Though she was a timid person, she was the first of her race to appear in the royal parks for a long while. Living in isolation with her husband, she hadn't lost all of the patriotism which the Loylars had formerly shared with everyone else; and she wanted to speak to the Prince's Nurse, or perhaps a nursemaid, since the notion of seeing the actual Nurse overawed her. She had her own baby along but, as she wasn't bringing a child for inspection, nobody dared send her away. Nurse and nursemaids had been dismissed to spare the two parents the sight of them and nobody else could answer her questions. The next afternoon when the Queen returned from a walk looking refreshed, the young Loylar woman was led from the pantries and presented. The interview hadn't gone on a minute before the Queen dashed from the room calling her husband—she wouldn't permit an instant's delay; he should come as he was, which was just as well since the girl was already tongue-tied without being confronted by the costumes of office.

"I can't tell you, Sir. He was such a small boy. He was only visiting us for a day, a good-looking boy, a little straw-head, poky nose," she kept saying bashfully. To the Queen it was written all over her face that the boy was the Prince.

"What was his pronunciation of horse?"

"What, Lord?"

"How did he say horse?"

"My Sir, we haven't a horse. I don't know how he says horse."

"How tall was he? Was he fat—no diseases at all—no scars, good eyes, no blemishes? Did he have his teeth in?"

"Yes, he had his teeth."

The King pressed away with questions with the furious energy he'd been giving the search in order to keep from howling in grief, but the Queen was silently certain this was the real thing. The shapes which the Loylar girl made, unconsciously moving her hands as she tried to find words, were the shapes of her son.

"Can't you say anything helpful? What shoes did he have on his feet?"

"Oh, he had just the sandals, My Lord. He was just in poor clothes."

"Who was he with?" asked the pale Queen, upset with herself that she was so slow in asking the obvious.

"It was a man. Not an old man, not as old as my husband, but not as young as me either." She glanced at the Royal Couple without seeing the example she wanted. "He was kind of a scruffy man, quite a smart man, but very poor. He could hardly pay for his food with us. We had to be giving with them."

"Was he a vagrant?"

"Yes he was that," she said. "He didn't tell us many stories about himself. Whatever he said you listened to but he didn't have much to say. He was traveling and he just stayed the one night quietly with the little boy and ate what we had to give him for supper. Then he went in the morning. I took the boy with me during the night because he didn't seem like a very warm-blooded man to me."

"You mean that he wasn't kind?" the King asked, rubbing his neck, as absorbed by now as the Queen, and his tone no longer so formidable.

"No, I mean his blood, Sir. He wasn't an unkind man, I wouldn't say. They were used to traveling together. He had a sling over one shoulder for carrying him over the miles. It was like a routine to them. They were settled to it. They weren't close, like a father's own boy, but they weren't unhappy together; you couldn't say that."

Emboldened, she stole peeks around the room, at the parquetry, the damask walls. Her own baby, whom she was holding, hiccuped and began to cry and she was allowed to sit down and cuddle it. She was round-faced and squarely built, with the slinky, husky grace of a peasant, and the Queen by comparison appeared blue as skim milk. But there was no relief in what the girl told them and the Queen was mournfully starting again to ask her about the boy's health, when the King interrupted.

"When did this happen, for god's sake?" He was annoyed. He was seated with his hands ticking each other between his knees and he twisted around to see which of his advisers might be in the room—that the most crucial questions like this weren't being asked instantly.

"It must have been a month ago, or more than a month. I'm afraid it's more than a month ago, Sir," the girl told him, flushing. "We don't hear the news, and life has been very hard for us lately, and I was afraid to leave my family and come and be silly in front of you when it was such a lorn little boy that he was, in no skivvies, even, or socks, just the wee feet and the little green shirt, and that not clean, like as if a man had him. I felt so silly even to let myself think that it might be possible. His hair was gritty."

Nobody spoke. The girl who at first in the Royal Presence had seemed to laugh at her own bumptious assumptions, to shrink and apologize, had now become guiltlessly placid, as though seeing the parents had finished her doubts.

"But what was he *like?*" the King insisted—to be so close to an answer!

"He was a good boy, very very easy. No fussing, I remember. He wasn't after what we didn't have to give. He was a gentle boy—only the teeth a little"

"*Look* like! What did he *look* like?"

"Oh, he looked nice, Sir. Very straight little boy, very re-fined." She dropped her eyes.

The Queen glanced at her husband. She asked whether the boy hadn't been cold in the hut.

"No, we had a birch fire, Ma'am. I think in the day it was warm enough for him outside when they were traveling. I took him into the bed, as I told you. I put him next to the wall where he'd be cozy, and of course he was having his supper too."

"He was hav—" The King swung around, and then a second time to see if a courtier had overheard. "He was having his what?"

"Oh he couldn't eat the rough food we had. We found that out. He didn't look at it at all."

"This is a boy practically five. Maybe we have the wrong boy here."

"Yes, he was that, Sir."

"Yes," said Janice, getting up, shaking her bracelets and touching a carved gargoyle head on the back of her chair. There were chairs for thirty-five people.

"He wouldn't have been able to hold down that rough beans we had. The chap said he had a delicate stomach and I knew he was tired from going so many miles—such a coat of dust on him. Such a dogged little gentleman he was, as if this was the way of the world for him and he knew it now, dusty, dusty. He knew what he wanted, himself. He was just waiting for me to offer."

"And so you—" The King gazed at the mother's own nursling baby. He was a fastidious man, not earthy and not a womanizer, which in a way let him accept the picture more calmly. "But he was weaned a good three years ago. You mean he had no solid food?"

"Oh yes, Sir, he ate a little bit out of the middle of the loaf, where it was soft, and we had a dab of meat somewhere that we could give him, but he couldn't have filled up on that alone. He had to have more than that."

"And you can't be clearer on how you would describe him?" the King demanded.

Seeing he was angry—seeing the Queen weep—she grew frightened and meek as at the beginning.

"Please, my Lordship, I don't know what to tell you. I thought he was a herder boy. I didn't know who he was and he was with us only the one night. I didn't watch him that much. He was a cute boy, a sweet little gentle boy. I don't know what you want to hear, begging your pardon."

"You don't remember anything?"

"I guess what he did when he wanted to go to the donniker I would remember. Is that something you would want to hear?" The parents nodded.

"He would stand in front of me and touch where it was that felt that it wanted to go, with his hand, so soulful. He wasn't much of a talker."

They went and looked out of the window. The Loylar girl lifted her baby from a pile of pillows. The King, scrutinizing her, couldn't pick out any fishy elements to indicate she was an agent—just a certain female sanctimoniousness.

"But he was safe when you saw him, you think?" the Queen murmured.

"Yes, I'm sure we took good care of him, Ma'am. Of course I don't know where they were heading. The man was a funny sort of a man, wrapped up in his thoughts and not very joking, but he wasn't a cruel man. I think he liked the boy in spite of himself. 'My friend and I,' he said, I remember, and he'd taught him our language. He was only a little boy that you couldn't dislike and they were quite used to each other. It was like a routine to them to stop for the night somewhere. He expected the breast. It was the end of the day for him."

Beyond providing her with a small purse of money, the protocol of what should be done with the young woman was a puzzle. She was lodged in the servants' quarters, since no one could quite see sending her home to her muddy farm, yet she wasn't considered employable. The problem soon was eclipsed by the sheer throng of Loylar ladies the police dug up who had similar stories. It was as easy as looking up all of the recent pregnancies. The Royal Couple withdrew from participation in the inquiry. If some of the girls were hiding a smile, most of them had acted from innocent charity, and though a certain amount of discussion did circulate about making a bloodthirsty end to it, Igor's was not a bloodthirsty country. The Prince himself was finally located, boarding with a wet nurse in a high valley.

The Chief of Staff was not in the slightest discountenanced by the fact of his future king having been fleshed on such fare. And the Chief Councillor gave out an announcement that human milk was a builder of heroes, that the Prince at this very extraordinary age had traversed the far corners of the realm, and that the Loylars, if they were perhaps a more rustic-spirited order of citizens than the rest, were rightful citizens nevertheless.

COWBOYS

Z INO'D BEEN THE GATOR WRESTLER since he'd left the Army last spring. Lemkuel's Hollywood was a pretty good carny. Offered lots of attractions but nothing too big for the trucks or expensive to use. Easy to move; played it cool. The hard part for the wrestler was hopping on him and off because if you know about gators you know they can't open their mouth once you're holding it closed—not the same as the muscles which shut it. That was when the gator's being calm was important. There's a powerful tail also, but this one forgot about his and, as it worked out, only had teeth to eat. Lemkuel told Zino to take some kind of spurs to him to jazzen up the show. Zino told Lemkuel to *hire* a freak.

Zino wrestled with the gator, and Spike, his friend, took care of the hyenas, controlled their jitters and made them laugh at the right times. The third guy who was with them, the paratrooper, took care of the carnival's elephant, gave the towners rides. He did a lot else and so did Spike and so did Zino but the point is they thought they were tops for handling animals, Frank Buck, Tarzan, and the cat's meow.

Lemkuel's H. was showing Kimberton while the rodeo went on. That's eastern Oregon, cattle country, pretty famous for its rodeos. Lemky's H. was there a week day-and-dating with the rodeo when all the people were in town. Wasn't competition, really, just to get their slough-off, which made a new experience for Spike and Zino and the Trooper, in hick country not to be the grand attraction. May seem silly, but it had to matter, working in a lousy carny, sleeping anywhere, with the numbers stamped indelibly on their shoulders in cattle ink they'd been given by the border cops when the show had zigzagged into

Canada to play the suburbs of Vancouver. Beside the rodeo, Lemkuel looked almost the same as the gypsy, nut-game, hot-dog stuff that used to creep up near his midway to try for a smidgin of business. And Zino and his friends were on the bum and not true carnies to whom a fleabag three-truck show set up in a vacant lot in Harlem, New York, might be the greatest object of attraction in the city: if the general public didn't know this, so much the worse for it.

Spike was a Marine—had been in the Marines—and he was sure he was the toughest thing God made. No, he let the paratrooper be an equal to him. But Spike didn't cotton to playing second fiddle to that rodeo. Competing cowboys owned the town like Lord and Master. Five-thousand-dollar cars wouldn't draw a glance if one of them was strolling down the street. Cowboys never brag to strangers, excepting ways like flossy chaps or with their hats, but even silent ways irked Spike. He watched the cowboys all the time. He'd squint. He'd reconnoiter vantage spots where he could watch a bunch of bars and several streets, and not ascared of nothing. A Marine.

They're suckers, cowboys, course. Zino had sucker stuff he fiddled with, Chinese charms, and they spent when they won—cowboys don't get salaries, they win or starve—so he had no particular complaint. He was peaceable by nature. But usually in a town people would be asking *him* and hanging round and being excited. Here, this town, *he* was s'posed to be the fascinated one and dog *them!* In a bar the cowboys would be leaning on their arms with all their weight, on account of all their hurts and pains, favoring one leg or the other, and everybody'd want to buy them drinks, breathe their burps, listen for the pearls of wisdom—when the cowboy'd gotten drunk enough to condescend to talk. Women would be saying those fancy shirts they wore were cute as mink. And, because of the rodeo, ordinary, everyday cowboys who never gave Zino any trouble in the other towns got to thinking they were special. Seemed to take an hour to make a quarter off them.

Spike wore tee shirts covered with the carnival and a mauler-looking leather jacket with LEMKUEL'S HOLLYWOOD CARNIVAL written out in full on it, the whole shebang, and always threw out hints to people as to where he worked. Here it was like he had had on a Wall Street suit. People thought he was different from them, all right, but they paid no attention to him, didn't give a damn. The cowboys weren't starting trouble, either on the lot or off it. They kept their fights among themselves— stand still trading punches till one guy'd run low, and that would start the tumbling over tables and the throwing crockery and chairs—bartenders were the ones they hurt, because they'd wreck a bar. But Spike lost weight about them, until finally Spike took Zino and the Trooper to the rodeo.

Zino'd served his time like anybody's brother as a draftee, not a Fighting Man. The gator wrestling redeemed him for the other two. And although Zino was proud enough of the carny as carnies went, he knew you had to be a bum to work in one and once he'd started getting some breaks from the world he'd quit—so in the last analysis he wasn't proud; it wasn't like a service outfit to him. But Zino was curious, wanted a laugh. He went along for kicks. Spike was deadly serious. Spike suggested it while they were hosing down the bears. "Let's *go* to the rodeo." He emphasized the "go."

"When we're off they wouldn't be showing either," Zino said.

"That don't matter."

Spike thought about the thing all Sunday, and the next day, soon as they finished the morning chores and before the opening for the matinee, he asked again: "You comin'?"

Zino hardly knew what Spike was talking about—"You comin'?" was all he said—and yet he really couldn't be excused by that because he had a notion. Even if he didn't know Spike's plans he did know Spike. Cowboys were hayseeds, Zino figured. He'd never been worried by hayseeds before, and if a carnie can't handle the hayseeds he'd better go straight.

"We'll see about Airborne," Spike said.

Airborne was sleeping on top of his elephant. He liked height. Spike didn't hesitate to wake him. "Hey, you want to stir some cowboys up?"

Airborne was down—fast as that. Didn't wait to be elevatored on the elephant's trunk. He jumped, and then he scratched his elephant's tongue. She moved it under his hand like diddling a lollipop.

"Do we got to clean?" Airborne asked Spike. Watching them was funny. Paint four dots on a piece of metal and you'd have how their eyes looked. Sergeants' eyes. Zino smiled.

Spike told him yes. It was risky because Lemkuel spotted people with nothing to do; it would be safer simply to clear out—in that the carnival was like the service—but they always made him wash. Being a good soldier, Airborne kept his clothes and face and armpits clean, but anybody taking care of elephants stinks something terrible. Washing doesn't do away with it, but you try. Stinks terrible if you don't like elephants much, which women don't. They argued about the smell and scrubbed and fooled around so long they had to call in witnesses whose noses still could judge if it was there. Finally let him be. No one happened to think cowboys must stink too; they weren't going visiting women. It was habit, washing Airborne any time they left the show.

So now they waited while he got his boots. He'd always fuss. Like putting money in the bank, when you brought Airborne you started off by sacrificing time, and Spike and him were buddies. The jump boots he had on weren't freshly polished— "These're getting crummy." His second pair was in an airtight plastic sack inside a box inside his trunk, each boot wrapped with felt to prevent scrapes against the other boot, and he was always changing boxes to find one which would "hold up." He blew at the boots to get off lint, then started in with rags and polish. Spike was sympathetic, but Zino told the guy to hang a sign Museum Exhibitions.

When Airborne was through with the rags, the boots were like you'd see on a colonel, and he was only partly done. He spit and used his finger round and round and round laboriously. Then to cement the shine he lit a match. The shine burned in, he took a razor blade and shaved the white-gut laces newly white. They were permanently put in, a special, raised, jump-boot pattern; zippers on the sides were used for getting in and out. He polished the zippers. Zino made faces and began looking forward to going to the rodeo very much. Spike tapped his foot, whistled softly, and stared at trees. Last, Airborne bloused his pant cuffs to the boots with two steel springs which shaped and made them rigid, and with rubber bands. A sergeant's shine, a sergeant's boots. Zino snorted.

"Are we ready?" Spike asked, trying to keep from being sarcastic. He sympathized with soldiering and didn't want to side with Zino.

"Wait'll I look, " Airborne said. "You didn't give me notice." Since he wore no shirt he centered his buckle and the fly of his pants with the line of hair down his stomach, and checked that the huge tattoo on his chest wasn't blurred by hair, was shaven: the head of a screaming eagle, his old outfit's emblem.

Zino kidded: "Did the gooks give you notice?" Spike still watched trees.

"Let's move out," Airborne said, satisfied and grinning. He snapped Spike a salute in fun, which Spike returned. None of this pussyfoot, brush-your-forehead-with-your-hand an officer would use; a leaping whiplash, an electric motion, an enlisted man's salute. They stepped off with the thirty-inch step, Spike calling cadence, all regulation. Hup Haupereep Haup. Zino was the slick-sleeve, but they weren't harassing him; he went along with it. Spike's lilt and chat and joyousness made it fun, as good as a band for stirring you up. Kosher sergeants: by the book.

Pretty soon Spike gave them Double Time, letting Airborne do the Airborne Shuffle. Spike was smart, though, and cut it back to Quick Time before Zino thought about the silliness of running; then to Route Step, where they walked as they pleased without cadence. He was a battlefield Marine and he preferred this, quiet and alert, not civilian walking. Put them fifty feet apart on alternate sides of the road with a stride that could last for thirty miles. And as he walked, Spike seemed to clothe himself in solemn battle-green, the aura of war, the time-honored burdens of pack, shovel, and littler gear and crossed, tall weapons—all half-joking; he wasn't a nut. But he started memories of maneuvers crowding upon Zino. The flares and hammering machine-guns; the trim traced mustaches of the officers; the clap of laughter when the top ones joked; the shadow of a marching file in the afternoon, long on the grass like a moving fence; the First Soldier during the hurricane telling them this was the United States Army and to feel some pride and quit their gripes, and late the worst night (not in the hurricane at all but when he chose to make it) standing erect on one foot in a jeep's headlights on a roadside post in his tee shirt and muddy pants and boots, telling the two hundred of them: "Yes, you men are troops now. You done good. I don't swear at men under me, I just run them till their tongues drop out, and the man that falls had better show me blood on him and whites for eyes, because I'll look. But you're men now, you boys, and you're troops. And any of you that were men before are good men now, and troops. You've earned your sleep. Fall out."

Spike said over his shoulder, "Fix your knives." His hand made the start of a motion toward where a bayonet would hang. He smiled, but his lips pressured together; his hands were dandling a weight—in his mind, by God, he was carrying a gun, and a man's-best-friend, not an idiot-stick like Zino's.

The rodeo arena was open-air, surrounded by stands, with a big dirt-floor shed at one end for everything to live in. As anyplace in show business, the way to the performers was through the most inconspicuous door an outsider found. It brought Spike under the stands and next to the chutes, and following the chutes he came to the shed. Airborne got fiercely bubbly, like the average sturdy sergeant about to be tested. Zino recognized the state and despite his own tenseness smiled. Spike was just alert.

"We gotta find where the crum-bums are hiding. What should we do, yell? Maybe we'd scare them. Maybe better if they think we're towners," Airborne said.

The animals looked to be out, the way they kept them. You could be used to the carnival zebras and bears and gators teed off and hyenas snapping and still not feel comfortable, seeing past a couple of grapevineyard slats those horns which even the steers grew, horns yellow like teeth, high and thick—long so you couldn't see both at the same time unless you stood back. Razor horns mellowed yellow.. The steers were packed in the pens so crowded that the horns were like a head-high mass of thicket. Then in another pen, instead of horns there'd be the horses' heads, goggly, watching Zino, all turned in one direction and touching each other, like a school of fish, hanging still or moving as fast as fish in unison with ups and downs and quivers.

The bulls were by themselves and didn't make Zino nervous; they plain made him sweat. Their pen should have burst just from the numbers in it—couldn't have forced in a pitchfork of hay; how were they fed?—not to mention the boards being about as thick as one of their nostrils. Zino'd have circled a field a mile across that one of those bulls was in—and watched awhile to admire it—couldn't have dreamed up a better bull in a nightmare. Not farm bulls: humped Brahmins for spirit, now standing as bulky and still as so many cannon. Twenty bulls in a pen the size of a kitchen. He dried his hands on his pants.

Calves for roping were squeezed in a pen like frogs in a pail and hopping and making the noise for everything else. In narrow spaces between the pens, besides the hay and cowboys' bunks, were dogs, cats, and special, privileged horses with blankets on their hinds and pails of water of their own. The shed held more animals than Zino would have expected to see spread on a whole horizon during a roundup. Right then, as soon as that, he felt sorry he had come. But Spike and the Paratroop were every bit as gutty, straight, and veteran-looking as before. They didn't bluff.

They kept a distance from the animals, not to excite them, and hunted for the cowboys, who were hard to find. Some were hidden in the horse pens, messing with the horses, and some were smoking in the hay asleep. Yes, asleep in the hay, smoking. These weren't the first guys Zino'd seen smoke in their sleep but were the only sober ones who didn't do it for a stunt and had the nerve to lay in hay. Another bunch was in the rafters of the shed with fifths of liquor, playing cards. Turned out to be the ones who at the time could walk without much pain, although their jeans were trussed against their legs for injuries. Zino and the sergeants watched them. Cowboys are really proud of two things, besides their horses and themselves—their boots and hat. And so they're always fooling with their hat, fixing it on their head or playing with it on their knee. And whenever their feet are dangling, straddling a fence or on a rafter, they'll kick them out, kick them back, and admire the spurs and boots from every angle. They wear dainty boots, with personality, pointed slim and formfit curving—funny to compare beside the Trooper's giant stomper weapons.

Dogs let the cowboys know about the strangers, but nobody was interested. Spike had plenty of chance to look around and map his plan. There wasn't much to see except the animals. Saddles on some sawhorses, a kerosene stove (banked in hay), and pots and dishes. Cots with Indian or khaki blankets;

saddlebags, knapsacks, suitcases, little private stuff, a mirror hung on the side of a pen. When Spike had learned the land, he whistled sharply at the cowboys in the rafters and jerked his rifle hand for them to come. They didn't stop to ask a question. Like such a thing was natural, they swung themselves around till they were hanging by their arms and dropped off down among the steers and skeedled out before they could get gored. The steers went wild. The steers thought it was raining men. The fence careened and cracked—but lasted

"They need some jumping lessons," said the Troop, meaning in technique. A cowboy pounded extra slats onto the pen where it was damaged. Zino noticed earlier repairs the same.

Spike played the situation fine. He took his time. He put his fists against his hips Commanding General-style and let the cowboys wait. Pat Patton's pearl-sided six-guns strapped at his waist would have looked swell, and a cowboy like Earp or Doc Holiday trash.

When the cigarettes burned near their lips, the guys asleep woke up a little. As this happened to each man, Spike jerked his rifle hand at him to come. The ones in fooling with the horses showed up of their own accord, propped on their elbows on an animal's back. Most all the cowboys tried to make it. The guys from the rafters walked, bowlegged and teetery on those high-heel boots. Others got a stick and used the corners of their feet or hobbled on their knees, arms crooked out with pain. A few only were able to crawl on a horse for the view and put braids in its mane while they listened. That's how to tell a rodeo cowboy from a regular one. Oh, the regular, he won't walk like you and me. But the *rodeo*, most likely he won't make it to the can without a horse. It's the falls which do it, not the actual stock. A herd of horses couldn't give a hogtied cowboy half a bump.

Zino was six feet, Spike even bigger, and Airborne, if a finger shorter, was muscled tougher than a shark. They'd murdered the loggers and the apple pickers and the sheepherders and salmon fishermen through Washington—there are no rougher places than a carnival. They'd have given the cowboys a day's work in a fight. But Spike didn't seem to plan to. He just was there to talk.

The animals got restless and stampy. But the cowboys were attentive, scratching their stomachs or tilting their hats around with their fingers, as they were always doing, or tinkling a spur; otherwise still and planted to listen. Spike had been practicing what to say all week, he'd been so mad, and now he had forgotten. He was confident, but he'd forgotten. Pinched his mouth and frowned. Each cowboy looked different from each other cowboy; couldn't treat them as a crowd. That's what bothered Zino. Each hat had its own independently airy-curvy brim, although always leveling sternly with the eyes in front, and its own variety of creases in the crown. And the necessity of hat-room made the cowboys space themselves so that each man was an island to be dealt with separately. And the faces weren't the same. Each had elements of its own.

Spike would do this kind of thing in the Marines, he'd said—on pass go into town and tell the locals what was what—but now the feather-tinkling spurs were all they heard. Spike couldn't start, and Airborne couldn't either, being out-ranked.

Suddenly Spike grinned, squared his chest, pushed his lips against each other and his fists against his hips, pulled himself so straight he was a picture. Loud as ringing metal he began.

"You people! Get this clear! Because your soul may still belong to God but as of now your ass is mine!" (The tone: why sure, he'd talk recruit.)

"The shit has hit the fan. I'm going to take the swagger out of you! I'll bring some order here. I'll straighten you. You'll take the course. I'm going to run you through a grinder! Each word I say is going to be your Bible. *I'm* your law and you'll stand tall! When I say jump you'll jump for me, you people, till you wee and wet your whiskers! Except you won't have whiskers. You'll dry-shave."

Knots and lumps stood in his face. He stopped and looked at Zino and at Airborne like assisting cadre, then beyond them to the pens of stock. The cowboys got the same expression from him as the stock.

"I helped put up the flag on Iwo Jima that the people took the pictures of; I was on the hill. I was in on Okinawa, Bougainville. I was in the Phillippines when the Japs gave in. And I know two things: Japs, they stink and you guys too. When I was going to school I hung from railroad ties when trains crossed the bridge. You couldn't do that now, but I was having fun and goin' to school. And I'm a better man with women." He grinned abrasively. "And I brought in the first Dakota well, my crew that I was in, which meant the state gets rich. And I knew Tony Zale like brothers. Not many guys have done the stuff I did, not you! Cowboys are for kids! Cowboys are for children!"

And Spike looked something fine. He'd dropped the boot-camp patter, but his tightened lips still carried fight, stamped what he was as sure as hash marks up the arm. His voice would fill a company street, and if he'd coughed he would have shouted louder. Those cowboys should at least have been set back. But no, and not insulted. They were enjoying Spike, hunched smiling on their heels like wolves sitting. They held their hats and tippy-tipped their fingers on them as if they had Spike in a jar.

"S'pose I yell Hey Rube like show guys yell. You'd be skinned!" He grinned at Troop and Zino to share how smart it was. Nobody's used Hey Rube in shows for twenty years, but he said that. They weren't near hearing distance of the lot. The Trooper, he was next to Spike's left shoulder, one pace out and one pace back, in shining battle boots, the screaming eagle on his chest.

Zino stood where he could make a run for it. Twenty cowboys to the three to them! But cowboys weren't the athlete he was. They're funny, cowboys. Blind drunk every night; chain-smoke, drink themselves blind. Because they only do the stuff they do for ten or fifteen seconds—stay on a horse—they aren't in good condition. Got no wind: never's a need for wind. And crippled. And always thinking about something. Watching you and sitting on their heels and thinking. These ones did. His back crawled.

Spike faced up to them, had suckled nails. "I'm from the carnival," he said. "Which means in every town the guys who think they're rough come down to make it rough. Everybody. Cops off-duty. And we handle them, *we* make it rough, we chase them through the town. I've always been with outfits like that. Our battalion used to trade the medics in for fightin' troops before we'd hit the sand. Our tankers emptied the tool box throwing wrenches before they'd die. No ammo and a Jap comin' in? *Give him the butt and the steel!*" he roared, so even the cowboys blinked.

He knocked the hat off one. The guy was bald. "Skinheads!" Spike sneered. "That's why you wear them hats!" He kicked the same guy in the foot, which made him howl. "Sorefoots! That's why you wear them boots! 'Cowboys!'" He spat the word. "I think they call you that because you look as dumb as cows. Huh? Answer up! Umbrella heads! Your cattle got your tongues?"

The cowboys grinned. Their mouths and noses got real wide. "Slaps, open up the gate."

Horses poured forth like a dam had burst, in a wall of dancing crazy water—brown as water—out the gate and racing to both sides. Zino bounced as the ground shook and the mass whirled round the shed. Singling out individual broncs was scarier still. They pinwheeled, their hooves topped their heads. Zino fell down in a ball and covered his head. Then he got up to try and survive. Spike was willing to run for it now, but too late. Zino stuck beside him like any raw replacement. The horses were everywhere, plunging and thrashing and kicking each other, fiend-faced, an oncoming merry-go-round brought alive. And now old Slaps got happy-go-lucky and let out a couple of bulls, which were charging but hadn't decided where. Spike couldn't maneuver because of the horses. Soon as the bulls spotted him and his men it seemed that they'd be cooked.

The cowboys didn't bother with the bulls, only to dodge. The cowboys were after the horses. Cowboys are cripples but cowboys can move, just never how anyone else would move and most of the time they aren't balanced steady; every few steps they'll fall. These guys were using their hands to help. Sometimes they almost ran on their hands, skeedling next to the ground like crabs. The slender skin-colored boots seen at a distance made them look barefoot. Several men had a funny run, limping on both legs: each step was a stumble and to keep from falling they went at a run. And as much as they ran they threw their hats, stalwart, sailing hats, so big. They must have thought it wasn't fun enough to rope the horses, because they dove and flopped and skidded, told each other wordless things and yipped and shouted at the horses, sailed and flapped and flung their hats to steer them. The hats were charmed, never crushed or tromped on; kept their gallant complex shapes, as if to wear one was to wear a helmet. Of course Zino and the sergeants didn't care about the hats. They were trying to save their skins. But the way to live was stand right still and watch in all directions. This they did, in the middle of the tumult.

By and by the cowboys got the horses circling. Couldn't stop them, but they got them circling, and relaxed, dusted off their hats with careful swats or with their fingers, and began to eenie-meenie, picking out their broncs. Everybody was inside the horses' circle except the bulls, who charged in and out. The cowboys took it slow, rolled cigarettes, listened to the hooves and breathing. Then they limped along beside the circle—a man might stop, change his mind about a horse, now go again—they stumbled along and one by one grabbed onto a horse's head like hauling in a running catch and shinnied up as effortlessly as rolling into bed—so easy. Course it wasn't. The horses sunfished, seesawed, wrenched around like puppets, and when the bulls got near went off their rockers.

A cowboy scissored with his spurs to liven up a dull one. Another man was having trouble, holding to a horse's neck, his body flat out from it like the greatest jitterbug. Got smashed against a post and really caught a case of the limps. Anybody else's legs would have been mangled. Once a cowboy sat secure, why he'd perch on the rump of the bronc, swing his legs up on its back and ride, with it bucking, like that, hold onto the hide with his fingers.

Mounted, the cowboys had some height. On the ground because of all their walking troubles, as well as legs bowed bad as wishbones, they seemed small. Horses became different too, more individual. Bucked tight jackknifes in a circle; or lunged roomily and straight ahead. Or the mechanical, classic, easy buckers, rhythmic as a circus horse, except the motions bigger. Affectionate horses acted happy. Complainers wagged their heads. The cowboys with horses broken fooled the bulls back into the pen.

Spike was catching his breath. He didn't seem to figure that these new procedures had anything to do with him. Airborne waited for his orders. Zino only wanted to be gotten out of what they'd brought him into. Spike watched everything, partly contemptuously laughing but also interested and entertained. There wasn't a trick he missed, hands on hips, scalp-close haircut, a Marine.

Still, some cowboys hadn't mounted, those banged up the worst. They crawled to the top of a pen, using their elbows for hands and their knees for feet. The rest of the horses were driven past and they got on that way, like straddling the chute. Men who wanted ropes and saddles went for them, and Spike began at last to feel outnumbered, started for the door, although to look at him he was a kid being dragged away. Now suddenly he ran—the three of them—a hard determined dash which would have bowled over anybody on the ground. Riders loped in front to cut him off and squeezed in from the sides and nudged up from behind. They crowded Zino and the Trooper in so close to him that the three hugged each other. From then on Zino never knew what he was doing before it was half done. The cowboys talked a different language, heeey*ah!* and wh*ooo!* and partly to the horses, and what they said was swallowed in the dust and noise. Their faces didn't seem to move, except the lazy smiles, so he never even knew who'd spoke. And he was running without stopping, the horses with their manes gone wild, and mouths, and hooves about to split his back. The dipsy lassoos teased. The cowboys doing it he couldn't even see, just occasionally, smiling lazy at their skill. Spike tried to slam a guy who'd been bucked off and they thought that was marvelous, as with some kind of monkey, though they wouldn't let the cowboy make a fight; it wasn't what they wanted.

The posse had no boss but one guy spoke officially. "Talk is cheap." He grinned at Spike. "You'll live, you fellas. Don't think we're out to kill you. Just havin' a little fun. Dusty up that fella's shoes. Do what you're told until its over." Which was bullcrap because they couldn't hear what they were told and had as much control of what they did as mice.

To start, the cowboys put a horse on either side of Zino and a horse behind him and ran him into the arena. Only place to run was straight ahead, until the horses turned him, and if he tried to stop the horse in back would stomp him. He couldn't fall down in the midst of the hooves, and couldn't climb the cowboys' stirrups because they'd whip him with their ropes. They had a race with Spike and him and Airborne—who could be got to go the fastest—although he didn't see his pals; was lucky seeing the sky. Yes, Spike raced too.

Then they cut it down to one horse and rider; made it like steer wrestling. Ran the man beside the grandstand wall and leapt on him from the horse. The hard thing was to land on target, instead of, when they'd do it with a steer, landing in the right position, heels braced out to plow the sand. One guy who missed Zino wrecked his knee; another struck the wall and was unconscious. And sometimes Zino had a couple of moments to fight them on the ground before the posse broke it up. "Don't spoil him," the posse'd tell the cowboy. Zino couldn't do much, with his breath knocked out; or else the cowboy would have hit the ground and be behind him. He slugged, ran, fell, was hit with those flying tackles off the horses, was bumped by the horses—once got hit with a horse's head; it tossed its head—socked like a club! His eyes were blind with tears of hatred and with sand. He gasped too hard to cry. The grunts of the horses pounding into turns and stops seemed to come from him. Knocked him down; knocked him down again; he gave up fighting, just tried to dodge and let the cowboys bust themselves against the ground. If, as he'd heard, the crucial qualities in battle were the wind and legs to run, he proved as well as Spike and Airborne that he could run.

Finally came a contest at roping and hogtieing. The cowboys who were last won because by then the captives simply waited for the rope exhausted. Even so, the cowboys fascinatedly compared their times for roping calves with these for roping people, and tried to rest them up to make it fair. If a cowboy missed two throws the man might run right out the other end of the arena and be free. Didn't happen, but it gave the roping purpose. And as much as catching the man, the cowboy had to put the loop to bind his arms or else he'd lose out to the stopwatch, busy in a fight before the feet were tied, because no posse would help him now. Spike and Airborne got some good licks in. Zino was too tired. A cowboy hung under a horse's belly while it galloped and roped Airborne from there. Zino didn't see. He reeled in circles. Always a goddam horse pulling taut the rope around his chest until the cowboy had him down and tied. Or else a goddamned horse's nose goosing at his kiester.

The three of them finished up as crippled as the cowboys, without the broken bones. Lay on their backs. The cowboys looked enormous from the ground, and the horses had tremendous chests and necks and wispy little heads; and tall—they reared and stamped—bodies huge and long like walls. The cowboys' hats blocked out the sky. Black sideburns spread down their cheeks and there was hair between their eyes; expressions on their yipping mouths to dream about. The chaps, the spurs, the boots, jean jackets, hats—each item never would need boasting. Zino didn't hope to kill the cowboys. He wanted God to have them die. One made a horse cross over him, kick near his head. He didn't pray. He shut his mind.

THE LAST IRISH FIGHTER

WEST OF TIMES SQUARE WAS a place sometimes to see show-girls in their daytime purple glasses and long pants. But all Kelly saw were two clean-cut nuns with boy faces, and a girl he'd never have known was a girl without looking twice, and a woman kissing her baby, and another one kissing her kid, and another, not kissing, but holding pressed lips to the neck of her child. A pigeon tossed a piece of bread like a dog with a rat, and a cat or a baby was crying, you couldn't tell which. A lady and a street cleaner swept side by side, until they got past the front of her house. Kelly lounged by the windows of stores. He watched a cop in a phone booth clicking the switch on a tiny fan and smiling so gaily he must have been calling his girl. And in the street he saw the white and smoky flitter-whirl of pigeons: the pigeons felt so good their wings were going as fast in spurts as ducks'.

On Eighth Avenue a card said GUARANTEED under every object in the pawnshop windows. The bars had their guaranteed drunks. The windows of the barbershops and greasy spoons began to show pictures of fighters, autographed and with the manager's address, and in a doorway sat a shoeshine-boy ex-boxer, his hands now agile and awhirl with brushes. That was what happened to your colored boys. But over a block, on Broadway, Dempsey had a big restaurant, and Kelly knew of plenty of other prosperous businesses that fighters owned. This was Boxing's Street, just like it was Pawnshop Street and Whoring Street and Get Drunk Street, although a wise man never messed with those last two. Madison Square Garden was here and *Ring* magazine and Stillman's Gym and the famous tavern hangouts and the managers' offices and the Boxing Clubs and

Guilds and Associations, Commissions, Corporations, Organizations. Kelly started feeling businesslike, like somebody going to work. He sauntered, though; he sauntered down to Forty-Second Street where Better Champions was.

The door to Better Champions Gym was marked by the guys outside it—not guys you would see anywhere. Some of them seldom went inside; just seemed to mark the entrance. Old posters lined the stairs, but since there wasn't any light nobody more than glimpsed them. At the top, by a window, was a huge white chart of ink on pasteboard which listed all the fighters whose fees were paid as of today and warned that no other fighter should attempt to enter without his money ready. Other signs were stuck at angles on the window, where you couldn't miss them, saying, "Pay!", and signed "J.D." Nothing had started yet and the managers and people standing around were watching who came in, and gossiping. It was like a judgment being passed, and Kelly didn't go too well, got blank indifference. He hated it and worried that the owner of the gym wouldn't recognize him as somebody who'd paid and would shout at him for heading for the locker room.

Among the quiet fighters changing, his uneasiness seemed silly. But even the other white men's faces were different from his, from speaking Italian or German or whatever they spoke, were shaped different. A Negro face—American Negro, not Spanish or British West African—looked like a countryman's. Nobody was much like Kelly. He was plain old native-born cop-Irish, without much Irish and without the cop. He snorted at the locker room. Dirt was thick. Paint had given up peeling; flap a towel, it flittered down like snow. Jogging in place, he swung his arms up over his head and down and rocked his elbows casually. He shared a locker with another fighter who hadn't come in yet, so Kelly had to find Peapod, the guy who kept the keys, a small colored man with a round wild face made wilder still by a wall eye. He was on a window ledge reading comics, but climbed in for Kelly quickly without grumbling, once he had been found. Hurriedly he walked, with short arthritic steps, unlocked the door and said, "Awright?" with such an upward, sidewise glance it might have been a word of treason. His eyes were full of water and shifted constantly, just as he himself did. After each time he spoke, he'd move away, as if he'd laid a bomb. He moved off now.

The wonder was that the door didn't fall when it was unlocked, with its broken hinges. Kelly sat on the bench, taking his time. He rubbed his leg hair. It was blond compared to the hair on his head, and seemed so thin or seemed so thick, depending on the way he thought of it. Creaselessly as gloves he smoothed his workout socks on, tied the high-top shoes—perfect fit for secondhand. His trunks too had been a bargain, but now the locker looked awfully bare with only the other man's equipment in it. Kelly had started to train again last week after a lapse of a year since he'd quit boxing the last time. He had no money and no manager supplying equipment.

"Peapod, I'm supposed to use that same stuff, ain't I?" he shouted.

"I didn't hear," the key man answered from behind some lockers.

"Huh?"

"I didn't hear about it," the voice repeated, sure enough, farther over. He must think, once his position has been given away, you'd lob grenades at him. Kelly's buddy had come, the one he shared the locker with, and Kelly looked disgustedly at him.

"Guess you got to go and talk," said the guy with friendly softness, thumbing at the gym. "And if you don't get any place you could try me, because I'm boxing today and I could probably let you use my bag stuff. You try first."

Kelly stepped over the benches cluttered with clothes and gear. The main room was full of gabbing groups. He looked for the manager whose stuff he'd used for several sessions by promising he'd spar with one of the manager's boys some time. The conversation in the group stopped for Kelly—for a stranger in civilian clothes it wouldn't have—but began again once they were sure they didn't know him. The manager Kelly wanted did a double-take and turned exasperatedly. "No, I can't help you. My kid isn't working out for a week. It isn't worth it."

"Just your gloves?" Kelly said.

"No!" He was sharp. "It'd be enough you use my gloves if you were working with my boy. I shouldn't have let you before this. Those gloves cost money. That's why you don't have none of your own." His mouth was as small as one of his eyes. Kelly tried to wheel away from him insultingly, but couldn't finish doing it before the manager had turned his back.

So what now? Sheepish though it made him feel, he'd have to borrow from the fighter. It was embarrassing. He passed a guy who motioned at him. "No manager?"

"Not right now," said Kelly. "I had Timmy Hannahan in Boston till he quit."

"How many fights you had pro?"

"Thirty-three. Won twenty-three," he added to stop the guy's sarcastic eying.

"Must have laid off a long time. You look old enough for fifty, sixty fights to me." The manager smiled. His large shadowy glasses sat on a large red face. His body was square and soft and his hair looked handled. His smile went through a lot of changes. "I'll let you use a pair; I heard the disagreement. I'd like to watch you work. I've seen you, but I didn't happen to watch. You seem like you could throw a heavy punch. From Boston, huh? Hey, Peapod!" he called into the locker room. "Give this boy a pair of my speed gloves." He turned and smiled and pinched his nose and blew it out the window into Forty-Second Street.

China was the name of the colored fighter who shared Kelly's locker—he'd been to China, maybe fought there. "I know how it is," he nodded, seeing Kelly chipper. "You feel like you own yourself again when somebody takes an interest. Then when they start paying your bills you know you do." China was comforting for Kelly to be with because he was older, one of the few who didn't make him feel far past his prime. China was over thirty and getting flabby, but, turtling into the shell he made of his arms and his shoulders, he did okay, even got some TV. Sharing a locker meant he could stash money for the future. He was wise.

The first people started hitting the bags—thunderous, playful bursts in passing just to announce their arrival. When the sound came into the locker room everybody moved more slowly, since they'd have to wait their turn. Kelly liked to listen and be lulled, like a connoisseur.

"All right, you got 'em! Don't ask me again!" crazy Peapod hollered in his small voice, glaring murder at the wall when he brought the gloves. China grinned with Kelly, scrubbing street sweat off his thighs before he put on his trunks. China's mask-like fighter's face was puffed up as from poison ivy or a month of crying. It looked sympathetic naturally.

A fly buzzed too long near Kelly and he brought his left hand from the bench and grabbed it in the air. Hand-speed was a talent. He slapped his mitten gloves together happily.

Better Champions was divided, half for the rings and half for the bags and tables and skip-rope space. In the middle was a huge, old desk with a big sign, "James DeJesus," and a littler sign, "Pay Me." A cushioned swivel chair went with the desk and a square was roped around them with the red-velvet-brass-post paraphernalia of a movie house. Kelly put his things on a radiator near a back window, where he would be out of the way, and began to fix his hands. He liked the job, did it carefully. The first of the strip of bandaging he put between his last two fingers and, holding it there, made four folds across the top of his knuckles. Then he began to wrap the strip around and around the punch of his hand, smooth and tight and supporting, and made an occasional excursion around the heel or around the wrist. He could have done the pattern in his sleep. It always ended the same. Each fold lay perfectly flat on the ones it overlapped, even when it went diagonally, and when the last of the strip was reached he tucked it under the front wind. From the second joint of his fingers to the wrist his hand was firmly sheathed. Tape he didn't bother with for working on the bags.

The wad of bandage for the other hand took a lot of shaking. It was twisted and getting grey with dirt, but would fit his hand ideally. Everybody used handwraps over and over, like old shoes. Along each wall boxers were doing the same as Kelly wherever they could find a space to sit their stuff, a bench or a candy-soda pop machine. Most had hotel towels, easily recognized from the next guy's, and were wearing shirts and robes; Kelly only had the towel. And exuberant ones were blasting a speed bag just for the roar, naked-fisted, till some Old Mother Trainer fussbudgeted over and put on their gloves.

With the bandaging done, Kelly felt like a fighter, hands like disciplined weapons. He flexed them, testing the play, and limbered his shoulders. He slipped on his gloves and gently tried them out against the wall. Rising up on his toes he started to shuffle. His muscles heated and blocked together so that he felt their power. They bunched easily, not too gracefully, with the catch that carried extra power. He felt tough, as tough as any middleweight he saw.

There was a guy over there who could sledge in a *punch*. He was steadily smashing a heavy bag with punches that would bring on internal bleeding. At the next bag was a straight-out high-puncher, two equal fists and nothing in his inventory aimed below the neck. Straight rights, straight lefts—all his moves were the same and carried higher than his own head if they missed. Kelly wouldn't want to be that specialized, but he could match the type, he reassured himself. In one of his best fights his opponent had lost his mouthpiece and Kelly had slaughtered the mouth so badly for the rest of the round that nothing could be done to patch it up. Next bell, it still was dribbling. The ref had stopped the fight. Spot-target hitting and plenty high.

The workout started with warm-ups, went to the big bag and the speed bag, and finished with rope-skipping, shadow-boxing, table calisthenics. Kelly was going to be third on one of the heavy bags and in the meantime occupied himself toe-touching and with setups and trying all his punches, both as he threw them and in the classic style. He figured little situations, punched accordingly. He feinted, sliding into his crouch and out and poising himself. He stretched from the waist in a circle, touching the floor, and in a shuffle pushed his fists up beside his head like horns. He galloped high knee-action spurts; back-pedaled, poking the tips of his hands down at the places where his feet had been; and limply stomped from side to side as in a comedy routine to use the muscles on his ribs; and bounced and bounced, scissoring his legs, twisting on them with deliberate wrenches; and simply stood idly and snapped his head in each direction to build resilient muscles in his neck. Then when the bell rang he walked around and loosened like everybody else. Three minutes and a minute rest. No matter what he did, how easy or how hard, it was organized like that.

"Where you been keeping yourself? Do you expect everybody to spot you?" he heard at his ear. It was the manager whose gloves he wore. "Yeah, I found a fellow who heard of you, but he wouldn't have known just seeing you. What do you think, you're famous? Maybe if they've heard of you in Boston still I could fight you some up there. No manager, you're sure?"

Kelly shook his head, formed his lips for "no." He crossed his feet with nervousness and rubbed his head. He wished he had his towel with him; he ought to use it between rounds.

"I don't know, I seem to have a skill, I don't let nothing by me, opportunities, I mean. The other fellow doesn't see it and I grab it up. Like you, I spoke to you. Nobody else even noticed you. I'm smart, I don't go sleeping, I'm watching all the time. And here you might be worth some money and I'm the only one who saw it. How old are you?"

"Twenty-eight—twenty-nine," Kelly said without pleasure.

"What'sat mean?" The manager leered. "Don't you know?"

"No, I know, I got to be twenty-nine a week ago."

The manager looked at the floor in sudden seriousness. "Well that might not be too old. Let's see you."

So he watched. Kelly wasn't doing anything; the new round hadn't started. But he watched. It was silly. Kelly was confused and didn't like him. His glasses had black frames which hid his eyes almost as much as dark lenses would. He handled them continually as if with pride, so that it seemed he thought the glasses made him better than somebody who didn't wear them. And his mouth was always moving, and he handled it and pulled the lip to show inside. When he breathed out loudly his face would redden. The bell set Kelly going again, but in the middle of the round the manager interrupted, "I'll let you have my card." It read, "Howard Straws, Manager of Fighters," and gave his phone number. "If I'm away the fellow next door answers, and I answer his, and we don't steal nobody's fighters. I can trust him."

The rhythm of the round was spoiled. Kelly fumbled through the last two minutes. Ordinarily he was confident. He had a solid, balanced crouch and moved without committing himself foolishly. He knew his shadow-boxing showed experience.

Ten guys bobbed and weaved near Kelly and each took up the same amount of space. Except for their styles only the names on their robes told the ranked contenders from the kids. The trainers treated them all the same. They spent more time with the people they were paid for by the managers, naturally, and more time went to big names, but they were nice to everybody and never deferential. The fighter they scolded might be anyone and would deserve it, but they didn't do it often. Little sad sacks the trainers looked like: they didn't change their faces or their posture, couldn't be excited. They'd trained the old-time greats and no one seemed as good to them as fighters of twenty years ago. Another reason was they'd fought themselves and had their faces bashed lopsidedly expressionless. Grave and pitying a badly beaten boy, they looked almost the same as when posing for an arm-up victory picture. They stood around and watched, a towel across the shoulder and a leather skip rope looped around the waist. As much as the managers talked, the trainers watched. It was their job.

Kelly started swatting a speed bag; the owner didn't mind. Stared up at, it was like a black bull's eye in a slicked circle worn by its contact with the wooden frame. He played with it expertly: tapped it into motion and its swing into the proper line, then pasted it smartly with the various surfaces of his fist and bashed it with a straight, life-lopping punch or an action like shotput-throwing. It was as tempting as a hanging pear. He tippy-tapped and got it swinging crazily, and then tick-tocked it. And all the time he pranced his feet, high-kneeling to the rhythm of his hands like a baton twirler. These were the bags that let the whole gym know what was being done with them. The groups of managers moved away, not liking the competition, but the trainers listened and chewed out loafers if they were concerns of theirs, or, if they weren't, told them to give the bag to somebody who'd use it.

The owner—one of those godawful wild men a manager had dug up from some ferocious slum—wanted the bag. He had a head like a pineapple—spiky hair and a brain that narrow. In the ring he set himself flat-footed and shoved stuff out. So he swung wild? So he had plenty left. An opening was blocked?

There'd be another. He pawed as if he were swimming, as primitive as that, and even on the speed bag shouted "Bam" and "Boom" and puckered his lips in concentration till they sweated. Speed bags were supposed to help develop speed and aim and certain sorts of stamina. The big bag built up power and taught you stance and how to set the feet and get off the punch. It was thicker than a man and larger than the target on him you could hit and, like the speed bag, working it was fun. Kelly's turn came and he nuzzled the bag between his head and shoulder, then rocked it away with a punch from the hand on that side and followed up with one from the other. On its return swing he caught the bag on his opposite shoulder and repeated the game. He hit the bag a couple of punches as fast as he could, and raised the number to three, six, always using just one hand, until both arms were weak. He hit it freely then, however way he felt, so that it swung in high lurches, and *whop!* he'd snap down, fists pressed ready on his chest, and let it swing over him, be up and lacing it when it had passed. He ran combinations— strings of lefts and rights in a certain order—or dug rapid-fire with one hand until he couldn't hold it up, it got so tired.

The last minute he lazed: nuzzled the bag with his shoulder and pushed it around like that, or openhanded it to get it swinging, and took his time, punching irregularly so it dipsy-doodled. He practiced twisting aside and guarding himself and crouching. He put his head in its path and dodged and ducked. After the bell he walked around to keep from stiffening and toweled himself all over roughly for the pleasure. Everybody did, except celebrity fighters who had a trainer dry them. But in spite of the crowdedness of the floor and the number of other fighters he had to change direction for, everybody was absorbed in their own training and trying to be as serious as if they were alone. Rope-skippers had a corner of their own where endlessly they flicked their hands—it would be training for a poker dealer—and skipped the strip of leather frontwards, backwards, right-foot, left-foot, slow- and triple-time. "You don't train for him, he take your head off," said a trainer, sprinkling water on the floor to make a circle for his boy to shuffle in. "He punch outside; you punch inside." And where are the hands when the feet go here? And learn the trick of falling forward to grab the crooks of an opponent's arms.

A heavy stepped under a frame and with a continuous roar blurred the speed bag to invisibility, an ideal-build heavy just growing out of the lighter weight, each pound put on to fill real needs. The noise got so great the trainers relied on signs. The bag didn't burst because the speed he hit it with distributed pressure evenly. Fighters usually killed the speed bag's rhythm with a Sunday punch once in a while to rest their arms until they started it going again, but this bozo batted it steadily for the three minutes, varying only the ratio of his hards to his softs— the pulse, the beat of his hands crissing and crossing stayed always the same. He controlled how hard he hit without the help of taking longer for a stronger blow, and his arms, at a peak of condition, needed no rest. Because of the varying force, he hit the bag at all points in its arch—it didn't go at the same speed, but was chopped into spurts which only a dead-eye could follow. Yet the noise he made was one noise without parts, a swelling and sinking thunder. His head led a charmed, miraculous life in the midst of his flying fists, and during the biggest racket Kelly was scared. This kind of a guy could send a hundred at you as fast as they could follow one another, all rocks heavy as your body was; sure, stoppable, one or five, but not a hundred!

"Hey." Howard Straws turned Kelly to face him, taking his chin. "You haven't done much yet, so I want you to quit and box two rounds instead. This fellow needs a sixty-pounder for his boy. I can look you over, and be better for you. How much you weigh?"

"One-sixty-three."

"Good. Feel okay? Won't be for a while. You got plenty of chance to change." He put his hand on Kelly's neck and steered him to the locker room. It was a queer sensation, having one's neck and face handled. Kelly had forgotten since he'd quit boxing, had to accustom himself again.

"Crackers will handle you—you know which he is? Well it don't matter; he'll know you." Straws slapped Kelly's shoulder. "He's a bum. I'll tell you confidentially they're all bums, every fighter here not counting mine. You look okay. Nice to see an Irish boy still fighting. The fans'll like that. There're not many like you—just Irish fans, no Irish fighters. We could bill you as the last one: might go fine. We'll see, we'll watch and see. Pea, give this boy my fighting stuff," he yelled at Peapod, and he took his hand off Kelly's neck and began making dirty-finger signals at a buddy, flipped a greeting at another. Then he sobered and straightened his sleeves and French shirt cuffs which had gone awry.

The last Irish fighter! Kelly's spirits sank. It was true: the Irish had gone on to better things; he was a freak. But right now coming to the gym fitted his life so perfectly—he was drawing unemployment and living snugly with a woman. It took so little time, half an afternoon, and a fighter got two thousand clear for network TV, after all the cuts, and being white and Irish would bring breaks because of the fans. He put a cup on underneath his trunks and removed his bridgework, and settled down behind the rings to wait, might be an hour. He sat beside China, who was talking with a friend, a studious-type sax player who came often. China went to his rehearsals. One ring was for boxing. The other was for shadow-boxers and was full. The flashiest show was being provided by a former welter champ, now just another tanker. No ordinary duckwalk: a bouncing spring-legged exhibition, hands on hips; he went like a frog. Did standing-up gyrations like a top. But throw a punch and he couldn't see it, and his legs and lungs went zombie-spongy in the first five rounds. Kelly was older than him, which was why China was encouraging. China still earned a living fighting and didn't worry about injury and didn't hate the sport and didn't always have to fight upstate—New York City fans would watch him. He simply trained gently and then went out and fought his fights to the promoter's satisfaction. Kelly's hopes were modest like that. Kelly loafed and wondered who among the twenty guys sitting on the bench he was going to box. Crackers, the trainer, was pointed out to him, a small bowed bug of a man.

The walls of the gym were painted black, but light reflecting off the neighboring buildings through the windows glowed benignly off the floor. Somebody's speed bag went like an outboard motor. The brown guy in the boxing ring put zing in every punch, dug them in like nails to last a century. All the power from his knees up and neck down wadded to his fist. No matter how far it had traveled he was adding steam to it when it hit. The sparring partner was jarred a good five feet by every punch; whatever he threw in an exchange he had to get off first. He was driven to the ropes and partly through and James DeJesus, owner of the gym, was standing underneath and jumped away like he'd been pinched. A manager next to him though, didn't, even put a hand up to support the fighter. Jim grabbed his coat and yanked him back.

"Always get away when they're knocked through like that, let 'em fall! Let 'em hit the floor instead of you, 'cause that's what they're liable to do, hit you. God protects 'em." Jim swung around to tell a larger group. He chuckled with soft sarcasm and grinned obscenely. "God protects 'em just like he protects the drunks."

"Easy, Luis," said a trainer. With each punch Luis' feet scraped the canvas with a vicious noise and a sharp snatch of air came out of his nose. Accompanying his punching, the two sounds echoed louder than the speed bags' roar. Now the pair touch-boxed, Luis in order not to hurt, his sparring partner not to make him mad.

Then Luis made gargantuan gargles with the water: mouth as big as the trainer's hand; his thighs thicker than his buttocks; his calves like shillelaghs shaped of muscle—so much noise and size and vigor that the water seemed still clean when Luis spit it out.

This manager of Kelly's couldn't seem to rest. Again he called him, into the middle of a group. Kelly crossed his arms and fixed his face to be polite and calm.

"Where you fought?"

"Where have I fought?" Kelly repeated, looking around at the jury of managers as Straws adjusted his glasses on his nose and squeezed his lips. "Boston more than any place. I fought in Boston Garden and Revere and Chelsea, Worcester. I fought in St. Nick's here as main event and I fought in your Garden once as last prelim."

"Who'd you beat?" said Straws. They all watched Kelly when a question was being asked, then looked away as his mouth opened for the answer. He did too, looked down at the backs of his arms.

"Who? Oh, I fought some guys that would sound good. But I didn't beat them." He laughed. He didn't make up stories. It was easiest to tell the truth.

"When was this?" Straws acted like a D.A. when he had a crowd.

"Oh." Kelly paused to think. "Not so long. Off and on. I'd start and I'd fight and I'd quit. Two years ago was the last."

"Well, you behave yourself." Straws tapped Kelly's cup to make sure it was on. "So what do you think of him, huh?" He put his hand on Kelly's neck. "You were all asleep, huh? And I got him."

The other managers shrugged noncommittally.

"Yeah, get in," DeJesus told two featherweights. He dropped a rock of rosin in a box and crushed it under his shoe and dumped the powder in a corner of the ring, banging the box on the canvas. He strode back to his desk, pausing to bang a window shut he didn't happen to want open. "I'll open the windows," he said grimly, picking his nose. The featherweights toed the rosin while they waited for the timer clock to work around to where they'd start. A trainer climbed onto the apron and gave them their mouthpieces, slicked grease on their cheeks. They went to opposite corners then. One took hold of the ropes and did knee bends, jouncing hard. The other hit his gloves together, readying them, and danced and tapped his headguard up so that it didn't block his eyes. At the bell they circled to each other so their backs faced away from the corners they'd chosen and their ties to them were cut.

Two styles: One guy hung his left way out loosely at his side and rocked it with anticipation. His right was cocked more normally. He was a lunger. The other put his fists beside his cheeks and close enough to thread a needle and darted forward, back and forward a few steps with continuous excitement. Of course in the midst of throwing combinations his fists didn't always return there, but it was how he began and ended. The complication of fighting him came from his nerves. He would choose his spot and brush his nose with his thumb and bump the headguard up from his eyes and start his little frenzied bobbings and the frantic seamstress motions. But when the open-fisted guy waded in to make the fight, the seamstress broke it off, sidled to the side and chose another spot. He wasn't afraid. He'd slug it out as hotly as the open-fister, but only when his jumpiness was stilled. Or else, another possibility, he'd work to such a climax of nervous and preparatory motions that he'd have to let fly.

Any number of fighters could use the shadow-boxing ring at once, and fast, because the real professionals moved fast. They'd done their rigamaroles a million times and went by rote. They pedaled backwards, caroming off the ropes and zigging in and out between each other; or slowly charged, launched heavy pulverizer uppercuts. Kneeing knees, kicking feet, shoulders shoving, foreheads butting—the ring rocked with a collective rhythm that the spectators could tap to. And there were no collisions. The kids went slow, attempted little, watched where they were going, but more credit went to the professionals. They missed a guy as skillfully as they'd hit him.

"Stay in, Chuck, 'nother round'll do it," a trainer told a fighter who was climbing out. The fighter grunted disagreement. The trainer made a face. "Chuck, you need it." No success. The trainer flopped his head disgustedly and threw the towel at the bench for the boxer to pick up himself.

"Whoa, Bessie!" came a yell. "What do we think we're doing!" A bulky man in a pin-stripe suit with his tie flying, watch fob hopping, rushed the fighter. "Gettin' the goddam hell out of the ring before our time is up?" He slapped the fighter twice across the ear and pushed against him, shoulder against chest, forcing him back to the steps to the ring.

"Okay! Yeah, okay," the fighter said and got back in.

"*Hey! Hey!*" roared Jim DeJesus. "I don't want no shoutin' in this gym!" He spat and his voice hit the wall in echoes. "If there was a woman and a child up here, what would they think of that shoutin' you did? Ya bum! Hit him again if you want instead of the shoutin', but *don't shout,* ya sonofabitch! It's *written right in the rules on the wall!*" He spat and strode around his desk out of control. "Sonofabitch!" He unzipped his fly and straightened himself and zipped it up again. He muttered comments to surrounding managers and spat again. His eyes swept round the gym and fixed on that one shouting guy as if he had killed women and children wholesale. Jim was scary, yes, but fighters had nothing to fear from him as long as they kept their mouths shut and obeyed the rules. He sometimes even seemed to look on them with favor, when they had been exceptionally quiet. Same thing with trainers, as long as they did what he told them. It was the managers he had his hands full with, unless he joined in with his wolfish grin when they were kidding. Kelly, buried among twenty fighters on the bench, could listen safely. He cushioned his towel behind his head and stretched his legs and laid his arms across his lap. Close his eyes or watch what rounds he wanted to; that was Kelly's "job." Not only got him out of the house, it couldn't be better.

Little half-pint chose himself a spot, brushed his nose with his thumb, went into his hovery knit-needle bit, elbows stuck out almost farther than his gloves, and waited for his man to come. But the other guy was slow; by the time he'd come the place had gotten hot or something for the seamstress and he'd strode away with stretching steps on ballet toes and taken his intent and bobbing pose elsewhere. Twice this happened, and the lunger, the loose-fisted guy who didn't bother with a guard, was feeling miffed. When he got there this time they mixed it up like so much scrambled cat. The lunger hooked his left up hard to bust the seamstress' chest. Again he did; again he tried. And down from up beside his cheeks the seamstress brought his gloves and stabbed lefts to the nose.

Kelly paced in order not to stiffen. Couldn't sit all day. Two tough middleweights squeezed past him with polite excuse-me's. Both were veterans—one's face was smashed level like a welder's hood except for his eyes, which had receded. They were through with the bags and carried their jump ropes, tapping the wooden handles briskly. And then they'd vault and shuffle in the shadow ring. The makeup of that ring would change from people who were starting the training session to people who were finishing. Kelly knew at least he wasn't boxing either of them. He wondered who, looking around the benches; several middleweights were waiting. He seated himself again and let his eyes half close. Straws was tweaking the chest hair of the trainers he could reach where it stuck out above their undershirts. When they moved away Straws yawned and turned as if to talk and was disappointed: nobody was near. His regular crowd was pushing around and about among them a small Italian-looking guy, also a manager, his face a meager version of DiMaggio's. They squashed his hat on his head for a joke and pushed him from behind whichever way he went. Kelly wondered how the manager's fighters felt. Finally they stopped to check their suits for wrinkles. Straws went to one of the groups which had just formed to tell the story. The members fixed their belts and smoothed themselves, their eyes shining from their laughter. They combed their solid-looking, molded hair and tried to coax the pushed one over. Straws opened his belt and tightened his shirt, spat on the wall and took out his nail clippers.

Crackers, Kelly's trainer, signaled.

"Ready?" Kelly said. Instead of answering Crackers snuggled the headguard over Kelly's ears and strapped it under his chin. He checked his handwraps and slid on the gloves and tied them with hard swift tugs; his lips bulged a bit from the exertion but otherwise his face stayed blank. Flashing a finger once down the lacing of each glove and once across the headguard's strap, he finished with a slight okay sign, and quickly turned away.

"How's this guy I'm fighting?" Kelly asked.

Crackers half turned and mildly spread his hands to indicate a shrug. He wasn't far enough around to look at Kelly, but he made the effort of partly turning. Likewise, his mouth opened: didn't say a word but opened partly.

"Which is he?"

Crackers angled with a thumb. The fighter was being laced: Kelly's weight, all right, little taller, but a good physique, light coffee skin. He wasn't a name. Looked tough, but who didn't? His trainer was drilling him some: small gestures and murmured words, working him like a machine. In the ring now was a fight of reelings and thumps; you wouldn't hear too many of them before a man went down. One man was fishing for the other's head and trying to keep from getting cut in half. He landed painfully on the other's eye and suddenly had no worries for his middle. A thicket of defensive whistling stuff was put in front of that eye. He should have changed his target then, but didn't.

Two cutiepants had the ring for a round. Always popping their hands against each other and making adjustments of target before they'd trouble to throw a punch; and little downward conversational sorts of glove movements like a couple of deaf-and-dumbs. And any time a punch missed, the other guy, instead of counterpunching, was sure to stop and catch the arm and make it continue its course until the thrower had been spun around, just for the fun. As Kelly watched, one cutie sent the other head-first into the ropes with a glove on his elbow and a motion like helping a lady board a bus. Kelly was experienced enough to know the tricks, but it was just hard on the legs and a nuisance, always being fuddled and spun and adjusted and having to cover yourself from punches from the rear. Revenge or maddening a guy was the best you could do with them. He walked beside the benches unkinking his arms. His opponent had started shadow-boxing, one hand fronting for the other like a bag. Kelly and he exchanged nods when they passed. Kelly remembered seeing him on previous days, but not how he'd fought, which was frustrating. Santos was his name.

They were side by side now in the ring, toeing rosin, holding to the rope. They walked again, with longer lunging steps and stamping as if crushing bugs. "Lemme see," Crackers called. He rubbed the grease on Kelly and handed up a mouthpiece. Kelly crossed himself because it would be foolish not to. The bell rang and they shuffled to each other, shoved their gloves out wary and wide to touch in courtesy, and took up their stances. Each kept his punches under wraps at first. Kelly was a stand-up fighter who cocked his hands for slugging, not to guard. Santos was a picture fighter, doing everything correctly, and he crouched. He looked impressive. He looked good.

Santos fought by the numbers: left jab and so forth. Kelly'd hook to the ribs to counter his lead—block it with the right hand, which he'd have to bring up, and instantly hook with the left. When the guy started catching those on his elbow Kelly countered instead with a looping right slammed over Santos' left hand as it came—didn't pause to try to slip it, took the punch to give one. The looping right was ticklish, positioned like that, but even if it hit his shoulder its power gave the guy a scare. He'd want a defense and was unprotected on that side. So Santos began throwing flurries, which meant Kelly had a chance to turn straight on and slug: Santos would stay there. And Kelly got to Santos, kept his flurries short. The guy had one of the best physiques in the gym, but his punch somehow didn't come up to what was promised. Kelly, as Straws had thought, threw heavy leather, but in a rudimentary, stand-up-fight-me, stoic style, and he was slowed down by being out of shape and old. To match Santos' flash, Kelly tried to punish, using single punches; this was his defense. His savvy partly equalized the difference, but he couldn't string together combinations the way Santos could—a lead with a cross with a hook with a hook with a cross with an uppercut to the face. However, Santos had no bite, and didn't look like he was going to grow it either, being already grown. Kelly: let *him* whang you to the gut a time or two with both his hands and he would bleed you, or at least that's how he'd been. Santos moused from lower ones, bending down, and brought his elbows to his belly. He headhunted, Santos did. Kelly roundhoused rights like swinging a bucket at the head, to please the guy, but Santos would move back. Hadn't tagged him yet, and Kelly felt the patter of his fists against his face—Santos must get mad, to land so many punches without hurting, although he was scoring points. Kelly did the coming in. Santos flaunted foot speed: let him flaunt it backwards.

At the bell they tapped each other friendly on the head and Kelly went to Crackers for regreasing and to have his mouthpiece washed. "Doin' pretty well," said Crackers. Kelly paced as soon as Crackers let him, too stirred up to stop for long. Felt like old times—and he remembered he'd been good—everything came naturally. He didn't sucker for this joker and he punched regardless. Many of the managers were watching—oh, not with worship on their faces; he could imagine the usual "Bum" being passed around; but watching, still. The paying fans who were here might clap a little at the end. They sometimes did. Kelly was looking fine, even against a hit-and-run like this. Well, he was better than a hit-and-hold; Kelly wasn't yet so old that he'd prefer a lover. And, to give Santos credit, he winged his left in well.

He likes to run: we'll run him in the ropes, Kelly thought when they began again. Santos was hard to trap. Once he dodged so it was Kelly went against the ropes, and Santos figured that he had him then and rushed till Kelly frightened him by lolling there, arms spread. Kelly grinned insultingly, but couldn't draw poor Santos close enough to slug. Yes, next time he did, and Kelly nailed him on the bottom rib and got a groan. He was the opposite of frail, but surely hated to be hit. He jumped up on his bicycle again and pedaled back, Kelly after him.

Such a clean-looking guy to chase. Tee shirt sparkling white, white stripes on his trunks, white laces, white shoes, white sock tops, purple gloves and new black trunks—so clean it made you feel like you were trying to mess up something nice. Kelly did a little better defensively, picking off some jabs like baseballs caught, and slipping others past his cheek and out of sight. His face was flushed from what got through.

The best bit happened at the finish of that second round, where it was placed most happily. Santos must have gotten careless. As he tried to duck as usual past Kelly near the ropes, Kelly reached him with an elbow and shoved him back. He tried again and Kelly grabbed him like a crate, both hands, and shoved him into place and uppercut to his heart. He fell against the ropes and bounced. And Kelly timed the bounce and uppercut to his heart. And left-hooked to his cheek, to show the world he could head-punch, and left-hooked to his heart. And uppercut to his heart. And smashed him on the heart. The guy pitched up and down and dove for Kelly's arms. He pinned the left till Kelly punished him so bad he had to let it go. Kelly battered at the upper belly and the heart. Santos covered up, but that was no defense. Kelly whammed and whammed, shoved him with an elbow to set him right and punched him on the bottom rib and left-hooked to his heart. And Santos pitched around and quit his covering up and dove again to catch the arms—pinned them momentarily, but Kelly worked one loose and hit the heart. And then the bell.

They tapped each other on the head and shoulder, tickled each other on the neck, as awkward as it was with gloves, and walked together to the stairs. Crackers gave them each a hand to lean on climbing down. Kelly's legs and arms were quivery. He couldn't seem to stop dead still. Aimlessly he strolled till Crackers grabbed him by his gloves and made him stand just where he was. He was like a child being stripped of stuff; he stared off absently, letting Crackers do the work, twisting his lips as a child might when Crackers took the mouthpiece out. Kelly was allowed to lick the sponge, but not to put it in his mouth. Crackers watered him and dried the middle of his body; when he began to need to reach to dry the arms and legs he handed Kelly the towel.

"Was okay. Course the man didn't hit. Hope you wouldn't fight with your face like that against some ones."

Kelly grinned. He scrubbed his sweat and walked, driven by his muscles to keep moving. He proudly glanced around at everybody to see how much they liked his stuff. He couldn't tell. Nobody even looked at him. Peapod from the locker room was searching the floor for cigar butts—not cleaning up: he smoked them in his pipe. The managers were chatting. China was boxing now, but complimented Kelly, clinching deliberately to have a chance to nod approval. There was a friend. Kelly was happy. The feeling of those final punches had been etched right on his arms. He was going to knock off twenty pushups on the rubdown table. He leaned against it for the shake and shake of the contortions of the fighters on it and flexed his hands and felt real good, real rough, real big. He'd plant one and he'd lobo anybody.

Straws was coming with a crony who wore a suit so shiny that you couldn't tell the color, whether blue or black or green. "Don't tire yourself," Straws told Kelly. "Listen!"

The crony started in: "I have a boy who's got a fight in two weeks, and if you wanna get yourself in shape too you can fight with him this week and then next week if you've done okay, I'll let you have five bucks a day for fighting him. Of course, he's better than the chicken-charlie you just fought. You wanna try?" He talked as rapid-fire as a sightseeing guide.

"Who is it?"

"Rudd. You know him?"

"Yeah, I'll try him," Kelly said. Rudd was a comer burning up the field, the kind that Kelly'd have to fight soon anyway.

"Damn right you will," Straws told him. "This afternoon. He's not fighting till the end, so you'll have a rest. Plenty of time. You relax."

"Good opportunity for you," said the crony.

When he left, Straws confided: "These crumbs drop tips. I never miss a word. That's how I picked you up and that's how I heard he wanted a boy to work his boy with. I don't miss nothing. Don't nothing these bastards do get by me. And another thing I was thinking was about this previous manager of yours. Are you positive I'm not going to have to buy you from him?"

"No, he died."

"He didn't sell you to somebody before? I don't want no lawsuits and the last thing in the world I'm gonna do right now is buy a fighter. Maybe he sold you on his deathbed."

"No."

Paid, no less! In one in ten of these bouts the sparring partner got paid. The money wasn't much—three-and-a-quarter a day, or less after Straws took his cut—but being paid alone would feel good. Kelly clapped for China and was partly clapping for himself. With China every defense move was utilized, and every kind of punch, very complex fighting. In the early rounds he'd rest along, and later when his opponent's defense became shoddy from exhaustion there'd be murder. China wasn't one of those old men so out of shape they tried for first-round knockouts, although he'd pick one up that begged him to. Kelly looked out at Forty-Second Street, the traffic, sunlight, sky. The sky was wonderful and big; the sun was fun, not hot. High up, seagulls sailed, so sharp they looked the shape of bats.

The Spanish-speakers' hair grew neatly long down the backs of their necks, while American coloreds as often as not had a wild scrap of hair back there like a pirate might tie with a string. Italian fighters were normal enough about the back, but grew their hair so high in front it doubled the height of their foreheads—which was to scare you with. What did the Irish do? Goodness knows; Kelly was the only one. The Irish punched. He wished he were acquainted with more guys. The Ecuadorians he couldn't talk to, and the coloreds had Harlem to gossip about. Besides, he was older—like the man over in the corner who'd fought Joe Louis. Louis fought a bum a month, the saying went, and this guy had been one of those bums— still scraping up an occasional fight because of the one Louis bout.

Two beginners were boxing now, kneading with their fists, safe distances apart. Their styles were full of fragmentary little poses they were trying out. When they did get close, they footballed with their shoulders and covered face and body with crossed arms until they couldn't throw a punch. They ducked too much and took each other's guard too seriously. From nervousness they let their hands, rigged tightly for defense, go out so far that they were useless both for punching and for stopping punches. If the youngsters did move fast it was from agitation. They'd flinch back even as they hit, in fear of counters, which destroyed their power. Kelly laughed; most anyone got hit; a winner absorbed better. One kid was still learning not to shut his eyes. And when the pair worked into clinches, without a referee to help, they couldn't come apart.

"Yeah, this is it," a manager at the door informed a Negro kid, and indicated James DeJesus. Jim had walled himself away behind his rope; he was studying snapshots, probably of relatives. The kid had trouble getting his attention, but then Jim listened, nodding in impatience at every sentence as if he'd heard it many times before, although not otherwise being rude.

"Yes, you're from Birmingham," Jim said, "and you came here and you want to fight. But where are you going to eat, where are you going to sleep, boy, huh? How?" With a motion of exasperation, "Pick him up!" he snorted at the managers who'd grouped around. They were the cheapest (including, Kelly noticed, Howard Straws), who didn't have their stables full. The first to examine the kid, a bald and bag-eyed man, made a fart noise through his mouth and lifted his leg like a doggie weeing. It was his favorite sneer. DeJesus had turned back to his photos and didn't seem upset immediately—he'd seen the act before—when all of a sudden he shook with rage and, stuffing the pictures into an envelope, went over the rope with his lead pipe after the manager, cussing his filth. The guy ran down the stairs ahead of him, and two minutes later was peeking around the door again like a child chased out of a playhouse.

In the shadow-boxers' ring a bunch was shuffling blank and timeless as a marathon except one lively kid who leaped and scissored like a dervish. The bookies' representative was there. The bookies pooled their information and only sent one man to sessions. He was easy to spot because he didn't dress to be conspicuous, the way the managers did, in bowler hats and velvet collars, and always kept a hand around his pockets checking on his multitude of slips and on his rolls of money. The hand that wasn't guarding pockets was used for feeling fighters. He'd wave them over, ask about their families and if they'd win their scheduled fights and what was new and what they knew and what was funny, laugh with them, and then rest his hand on them and slap them to congratulate them that their health was fine. Meanwhile he'd be feeling muscles in their arms and shoulders and the special muscles in their necks which might absorb the K.O. from a knockout punch. Legs he'd judge by eye as often as he'd squeeze them. When he was through he'd stop and make a mental note of his appraisal, pick his teeth.

Standing in the door was a young light-heavyweight with face not yet in the final fighter's mask. He was in his best suit, preened, and leaving to box on the coast, Kelly'd heard. He carried his suitcases too easily to notice right away. He seemed afraid to enter his own gym without being welcomed, the bashful, gawky stance trying to be so suave. He was afraid because of his suitcases and best hat, best suit, best shoes, so vulnerable to being poked fun at, his very, very best, stripped of all excuse. For another reason, his wife was lingering in the shadows with their baby son. She was timid-looking, black like her husband, and had come to see him off. When the fighter did move into the gym he shambled. His legs couldn't keep up with his body and his head bobbed, his arms waggled ludicrously out of rhythm, not because the suitcases were heavy, but because he was scared. Kelly was impatient. When Kelly slicked himself up in his traveling clothes he didn't fall to pieces and go bashful; he was cool.

The light-heavy's manager greeted him and shook hands with the wife, told her how swell her husband was and praised the son. The light-heavy edged to the side, smiling with embarrassed pride. He set his suitcases down and clasped his hands to keep them out of trouble, planting his feet stiffly. The bookie wished him luck and he tried to stay alert and bright for whatever might be wanted of him. On top of the shyness, though, an excitement sang in his expression. This type of guy didn't leave his neighborhood except to box; and now there'd be the taxis, the airports, cross-country flights, hotels, the big shots patting him, swank restaurants, and TV cameras and newsmen and the arena mob. In the newspapers you read sob stories about Negro ex-champs—how sad it was that Beau Jack, the gallant lightweight of the Forties, should be a shoeshine boy. Should Beau Jack have been a shoeshine boy straight through instead, and never been Beau Jack at all? And was it better that Joe Louis owed the government a million after being the greatest modern champion for thirteen years, or for Joe Louis to have spent his life in Detroit's Browntown heaving coal?

One event the fighter insisted upon. Again and again he looked at James DeJesus until his nerve was up, then touched his wife so she would follow. Jim acknowledged the trio by jerking his head for the guy to speak, not rudely, but to the point. It was his way with fighters. He didn't make them speak up loud, like he would managers, and for shy ones he would lean his ear much closer than he'd lean it to a manager's mouth.

"Mister DeJesus, I'd like if you would shake hands with my wife so she would know you," the light-heavy said. "This is Mister DeJesus. He runs everything."

Jim courteously responded, even to admiring the child, and would have slugged a man who cursed, but finished soon enough to show he took it as his job. He spat on the floor during the interview, but that was nothing—he'd have done that talking to George Washington. Children of white fighters he would often kiss with that same spitting mouth.

He was concentrating on his photographs again when, hearing one of the managers say hello on a pay phone more than once, he felt obliged to give some lessons.

"You can do it however way you want," he started gently. "It don't kill me. I'm only telling what I think is wisest." Pacing up and down beside the booths, he waited for a call to demonstrate. There was one, and he whirled and sprang for it. "Better Champions!" he snapped. . . ."What?" Instantly he slammed down the receiver.

"Now there was a case," he lectured, "where the party did say something, but I couldn't hear what it was. If you can't hear him you can't talk to him, can you? So hang it up." Jim grew enraged. "If he can't make you understand him, he don't know what in the hell he's saying! If he don't speak up with his business quick, hang him up! He don't have no business! Maybe might be the wrong number! Hang him up!" He raced into another booth which rang. "Better Champions!" he shouted furiously and slapped the receiver back again. "That was a different case," he told the crowd of managers. "I couldn't hear the woodhead; I couldn't hear a thing. It wasn't that I couldn't understand him, I couldn't even hear him!" The idea flabbergasted Jim and he turned logical: "And who would want to call you bums but bums anyway? And what do you want to talk to a bum for when you got so many here? Who else is going to call you? Only a bum would call a bum. Hang up quick."

In the ring a beginner sprawled against the ropes, taking a thousand and never trying to clinch or get away. Feverish, holding his breath, he pawed and pummeled back. Every kind of fighting style came off the street. The other guy was sinking 'em in with long snake arms and myriad spidery feints. But the more he hit the beginner, the more the beginner tried to hit back. That was guts; now give him a trainer.

Rudd, whom Kelly was to fight, was listening to another fighter. "I told him right in front of the ref, 'You keep on running on me and I'm going to stand on your feet to hold you still till I can slug you.'"

Rudd listened with a real respect. His answers were too soft for Kelly to hear, except for the Negro-backsticks accent, but he understood when Rudd shrugged with his hands to get out of talking. His weight didn't spread into height like Kelly's, and his arms were short, but all of him was muscled as machinely as a fish. Kelly nodded and Rudd nodded back from politeness, obviously not knowing who he was. A modest face, but awfully flattened, and his career had only begun. His nose seemed to cover the front of it, dwarfed his mustache. Kelly felt his own nose. The thickening couldn't be ignored, but he laughed because a manager had kicked another in the seat and started a slapping bee. He fidgeted his hands to keep them off his nose. That didn't help enough, and finally he had to walk. Walking started him thinking how his muscles felt and balling them and stretching. He wanted to do well.

"Well, we'll see if this is glass." Straws, switching on a smile, tapped Kelly's chin, although his eyes were searching him. "But he don't let his legs do nothin', he don't learn. Fights almost pier-six."

"You hit him, he goes down, he hits you, you go down?" Kelly asked.

"No. He don't go down." Straws squeezed Kelly's chin. "You can jab him silly—not what his manager wants you to do, but there is sure to be somebody in in the next two weeks who puts on shows and I can give the sign to jab and we might have ourselves a bout. If you're good against Rudd, they'll give you one. We'd lose the little money and we'd make the big." He made a face and shoved his fist at Kelly full of threat. "Get him!" Kelly walked away. They tried to put across to you how much tougher they were—tougher—how superior in every way; wouldn't even leave the fighter that.

The Number Four Contender of the Welterweights, and Kelly's favorite fighter, hopped into the ring: favorite fighter to watch; he'd never spoken to him. Usually the guy used bags, and so to see him was a treat. He'd whip his body up and down and pump out punches fast as Kelly'd tap a finger. He both started and finished exchanges and always knew what he was after. He'd paste your facial openings shut and leave you sorting out your parts. From the country of Colombia, he chuckled Spanish to his sparring partner, and through the mouthpiece it emerged monkey yunks. Number Four's equipment was in nifty piercing reds and greens. He himself was chocolate-brown, a well-formed five-foot-nine. And what a face he had—eager, mild, unmarked, an unhurt nose. The man in with him was a little younger, maybe twenty-one, and jounced his warm-up footwork with a consciousness of being outclassed. His crushed face was merry as he returned the jokes. Their grins were each distorted by the mouthpiece, but Number Four's was less so. He let his upper lip slip up until he looked as though his mouth were full of gum.

They blocked their arms out in a box for touching gloves, touched elbows too. The partner's style was raggedly gutty and wasteful, composed of constant straight-out pushes trying to wear his adversary down. So Number Four gave him the same—rifled level breastbone shots with longer arms. Then Four softened—didn't want to discourage the guy with his own stuff—switched into more natural ways, and pushed the partner gently back when he got in too close for Four to bomb him. If the guy insisted upon pressing close, why Four'd collapse and lean on him with all his weight until in a bout the ref would have had to break them. Or, if the partner hunched low to escape the stoning, Number Four would simply lean down hard across his back, trapping his neck in an armpit, until, again, a referee'd have broken them. In between these sapping clinches he romped out punches in assorted styles, hooks, jabs and upward-movers—uppercuts and golfed-in bolos—and crossed his arms to stop the counters, grinning when the other guy threw stuff because it opened him up the more for attack. Of course Four didn't need an opening to punch. He whacked 'em in, openings or not, hit the biceps if that's all there was, but hit and hit, hit and hit; befuddle the guy and fox the judges' eyes. Down he bent and up, chop-stepped, and shook the golden talisman that hung around his neck into a fling. His body almost rubber-shimmied in exigencies of golfing blows and of defense. But it looked easy. As part of readying his own, it seemed, he picked off punches, as breezily as that. Real horse-hoofs: tucked 'em in his palms. And when he slipped a punch you'd think he'd glanced across the street, so simple and so neat. Just casual. Or as if in a rhythm. And all the time he pumped in punches quick as sharks.

The partner naturally had got depressed. Number Four dropped his arms, quit offense and when the guy let loose his all, just wriggled with delight at the massage. And rocked against the ropes to hear them creak, rocked and rocked, began avoiding punches with his body, curling kitten-wise this way or that, sucking in his tummy; arms stayed at his sides. Around the ring like rubber he rocked, limp and lax and scarcely getting hit. One rope's spring propelled him to the next. Eluded and evaded everything as if it were rehearsed.

He stopped that business, took a few and let the guy get to him and raised his arms and fought in close. He fought like you would see him on TV against class fighters at their best, who'd have their way to some extent, Four unavoidably being hit and thus sharp-punching at tight targets like the nose and eyes and solar plexus to cut and pain the man and jar his aim; of course he'd hit the jaw whenever he could. This guy wasn't quite the same, though, this poor kid with features bull's-eyed in a wad. Number Four drained everything to quarter-strength for him.

And on Four's face that mild, eager searching look like always when he fought.

He frauded for the fun of it now, Four, pretended to be hurt and woozy—buckled knees, drooped head. He 'possumed helpless in the middle of the ring, fumbling for a clinch, woodenly walking into what was thrown, exposing his heart and tummy. But as the partner got engrossed, Four sharp-shot a bunch of aces to eyes and nose—kept quarter-force—and by mistake, it must have been, he clonked the partner's chin. This put the sags and staggers in the partner's legs; he braced them wide-apart and quivering. Number Four put out his arms as stiff as railings for the guy to rest on and, when he could stand up by himself, just nuzzled languidly head to head with him and slowly shadow-boxed, leaving his own stomach open-target for encouragement.

When the guy felt better Number Four spoke Spaniard to him, apparently telling him he'd let his face alone, to cover up his trunk. The partner crossed his arms. Number Four whipped golfing bolo rocket punches down from shoulder height which smashed in on the navel, real divine whirlo bolo punches arching like a scythe which made the paying fans shout. Show-off, yes, but full of zazz. Little Peapod paused in hunting cigar butts to watch. His eyes, instead of being muffled with subservience, were lighted fiercely.

They wrapped their arms around each other's shoulders and went to get rubbed down. Both faces gabbled Spanish happily—Four Contender's mild and eager, the partner's like a penny put under a train.

Shuffling, Kelly wrung his wrists and rolled his head around on his neck like a juggled ball. He fiddled with his trunks to sit them higher on his midriff so the legal target would be lessened, and wiggled his feet—the socks were smooth, the laces tight—and closed his eyes, rested vacantly. For a while he was just conscious of his body, how comfortable it felt, not springy like a kid's, but plenty big and tricky. No, he wouldn't be hurt, he felt too fine; he was in his prime. Good old boy that never gave him any trouble. He found a private corner behind the rubdown tables and looked across the straightening-bending bodies to the whole of the gym. It was a madhouse. In the ring a skinny fighter was taking a beating. Every time he got off something the sound would show he'd hit an arm. Every time the other man chopped in his right there'd be the soft thud of hitting home. The ring shook and squeaked. Spectators clapped. Shadow-boxers stomped the floor. Skip ropes slapped and whispered (when you couldn't hear them, watching them you thought you could). The skippers thumped their feet. Big bags jerked and shivered up at crazy angles, to the thunder of the little ones. Fighters shuffled in a maze of warm-ups. Several languages were used. The managers goosed and sparred hilariously, pulling ties. "Who?" DeJesus yelled above the uproar; a name was wanted on the phone. *"Who? Cufflinks Prince?"* He gaped with disbelief and leapt up, spitting like a hot frying pan. He would have thrown his arm except it was attached. *"You know that bum's not allowed in here!"* His two poor legs hardly could support his fury. He hawked a real whopper up and let it fly. From the fighting ring, sharp anguished gasps and snorts of heavy labor; the blinks were in the skinny fighter's eyes, his head was being knocked back and forth with faint flesh-squashing noises as fast as if it were a bag. It shivered like a melon, unattached to him, and flung off hair sweat, tiny tears and spittle drops which could be seen. His headguard looked about to split—it looked as though the lacing of the headguard was lacing on his very head and couldn't help but split. And still the punches came in succinct thuds. Speed bags reverberated savagely through the gym and underneath their roar were sounds of shaking rings, DeJesus' fury, managers' catcalls, whizzing skip ropes, shadow-box gyrations, heavy bags being plastered, plunging calisthenics, until the gym seemed about to fly apart.

Rudd paced as though his rounds were soon. Kelly asked him, "When do we go in?"

"Are we boxing? I don't know, when they tell us." Rudd pointed at a doe-eyed Negro. "I've got him too. He might be first." He paced alongside Kelly companionably but silently, looking at the floor. Their strides weren't matched. Rudd seemed to churn along with tremendous energy, slow and channeled. Even walking, his legs hardly stayed under him; they were geared to driving ahead so powerfully. Fighting, if he didn't come on at you, he'd fall flat. Kelly'd watched him on TV against a classy boxer-puncher tiger who assumed a fancy stance and moved in like the dreadnaught that he thought he was. Rudd, also moving in, had tagged him twice; and all the offense and the class went sick, the tiger dropped them like a stone to cover up and bob down in his lowest crouch. Rudd chased him till he'd knocked him out. His face was scary to anyone who cared about his own: it had a dozen widgets from sewn-up cuts and over parts of it a slick scar-skin had grown in place of welts, a skin so shiny that if he'd been white it would have looked like bone. Under the skin-thick reinforcement buttressing were eyes swollen into Oriental slits, cheeks Indian and huge, brows, nose, chin, each immense—that was what you punched at, features. When Rudd had first puffed up he'd probably looked like China, permanently crying, which made a funny contrast with a smile. But now he'd gone beyond that. He just looked puffed, as with weary sleeplessness, no emotion, only puffed. And his nose, although gigantic as three noses, had been leveled down until it was becoming just another buttress pad across his face. Twenty-two Rudd was.

This was no way. Kelly went off by himself again to get into a better frame of mind. He was still in his twenties and younger than plenty of active champs had been—what did he have to worry about? He'd sparred with Tony DeMarco when both of them were kids in Boston, and Tony had ranked Number One behind Basilio for years. Kelly slipped into his fighting stance, arms set loose, hands quite wide. It was a good reliable stance for any general purpose and boosted his spirits because he was proud of it. He really began to feel like fighting. It was a mood to be worked into by walking, by getting grim, thinking what Rudd hoped to do to him and what the rounds could mean if he did well and what specific punches he was going to throw. Soon he was ready to knock the stuffing out of anyone.

Five minutes later he munched the mouthpiece out of Cracker's hand and slid his shoes around, looking solemnly down on the people. "To the meat," Rudd's trainer was telling Rudd. Kelly smiled and bit his mouthpiece sternly. More than the gloves, the mouthpiece in his teeth made him know that he was going to fight. He crossed himself and circled the ring, dancing and thrusting out his arms. A grave and blank expression settled over his face to cover up the rising heat he felt. He went to a corner and faced away as if Rudd's name were being announced, ground his feet like crushing bugs, plotted how his arms would go. Twice he glanced at the clock, and ticked the time off in his mind, turned as the bell was about to strike and scrabbled a cross in case he hadn't done it right before.

Most anybody would exchange hands at first, a lead for a lead, a cross for a cross, in a study period, but not Rudd. He probably couldn't lead, he was so crude. Plod and halt, plod and halt was his pattern—halt if he could drag his legs underneath him fast enough. His gloves pointed at each other by his stomach, making no defense attempt. Kelly jabbed him as Straws had suggested and the reaction was an uppercut one-two, the right hand's path a mirror of the left's. Neither got to Kelly; he stepped back. Rudd, ungainly guy, hadn't any follow-up or plan—jabbing him you might as well have pressed a button which turned out uppercuts and roundhouses and looping overhands; the last two he threw only in excitement. And the side of the glove seemed the same as the punch of the glove to him. He didn't care. Everything went all out. Everything was spadework for a K.O. He had no subtleties or medium attack.

Kelly put his hands further from his body than usual and hit Rudd with straight things to keep him off—not that it bothered Rudd so much, but his arms were shorter than Kelly's. He was the opposite of a counterpuncher, being entirely aggressive, but he acted like one with those automatic uppercut answers to each of Kelly's jabs. He had a horseshoe in his glove—Kelly's forearms caught the uppercuts and even there they hurt. Kelly warmed more to the round and stung Rudd with a combination to the head which at least made him lift his arms. The next one he sluffed aside like a snowplow, as elementarily as that. Kelly grinned across his mouthpiece at Rudd's crudeness. Pretty soon he'd quit this caution and slug naturally, working from the body up. He winged a straight long left to Rudd's mustache and curved a right which ended on his eye and dug a left hook to his heart. All went through.

It seemed like he could score at will, because Rudd's arms were down. What doing? Kelly's belly almost left him, that's what! The second uppercut—no aim adjustment made for Kelly's doubling up—hit Kelly's chest. The third, immediately after it, from the left hand again, would have rubbered Kelly flat except he stumbled to the side. Instead of his chin it hit his shoulder. He was way down, face gargoyled in pain, clutching his arm across his middle and trying to pry his head in underneath them. He couldn't have stuck his arms out for a clinch, his belly was too caved; it hurt like a vicious cramp. He quavered backwards as though on ice, groping with his feet. Rudd kept throwing, misses because Kelly had moved, sometimes roundhouses instead of uppercuts, although the arc made was the same. Ponderous, Rudd pushed after Kelly, but Kelly could go faster and gradually recovered, his cockiness not wholly scared away.

What a funny fighter! Western-movie-type: no punching volume, only force in what he threw. The trainers had accomplished nothing except stretch him out to go ten rounds. All that remained for them to do was give him his feet and a guard and teach him to lead and to hook and to jab and to cross! Kelly would stick him with jabs, and there was a sneak straight right he'd called on in the old days, and his rainbow right brought down from the sky. Powercrazy Rudd with his windmills from ten feet out should be no permanent problem—he didn't even seem to keep track of where his own hands were, but would sort of discover them before he punched. Ugly, octopussy style. Kelly hung out of Rudd's range and sent him stuff which had gone soft by the time it landed. But he reached his eyes. After all the receding they'd done and the cartilage surrounding them, still they could be reached, and got their corners cut each feature bout. Kelly'd frame a mouse around both eyes.

When Kelly came to closer quarters, Rudd began to shove. Strange shoves, the purpose not to set up Kelly for a punch, but to set himself! Kelly was a sack of something to be lifted, and all Rudd thought he needed was the leverage. He'd try to tip him in the right direction with a shoulder jostle and put his head against his neck and place his feet, and then let blast; of course Kelly wouldn't have it go that far, and Rudd was anything but hard to fool because the fact of Kelly's being a human, not a sack, came as a surprise. Blocking those uppercuts was murder on the wrists and elbows, though, and once when Kelly grabbed Rudd to tie him up he found he couldn't hold him—he couldn't clinch! So what to do, stand and trade blockbusters with the guy, or spar and run and guard his health? He had no choice. *That* missed Kelly, and *that* did too, thank God, and Kelly landed one, he thought. But Rudd was happy to take five in order to throw two. Rudd lurched, ape-footed, heaving up his paws. On TV when his man was macaroni on the ropes he'd go into a wild and stamping dance with punches flung exultantly as whoops. Study him, study him, Kelly told himself. He was giving up the possibility of looking very good. Cautiously he held him off. Rudd was familiar with delaying games, but he didn't make allowances for them, didn't even get mad. Mad, he couldn't have swung any harder. "Work, Charlie! Mix, Charlie!" yelled a fan. Kelly backed away, thankful Rudd was slow. He tried again to tie him up. The arms that clung onto Rudd were no stronger than two noodles; into his stomach big bombs burst. He got away sick with pain. To fight a guy he couldn't neutralize by clinching was terrifying. Hit him and run, hit him and run was the only way to last, and Rudd had learned Kelly's rhythms now, such as they were, and went after him quicker. Kelly was trapped and hurt twice in the corners right in the belly. He couldn't punch free. He pulled himself out by a rope one time, wobbling in pain; the next he caught hold of Rudd's head and tried to bang it on a ring post. Rudd's trainer shouted angrily.

They tapped each other on the head and on the fanny at the bell and circled the ring in opposite directions until they came around to where Rudd's trainer stood. Kelly leaned on the rope, exhaustedly resting. The trainer would have lagged with Rudd, but Rudd wouldn't let him, made him give Kelly attention. Kelly's nose, cheeks and forehead were regreased, also his gloves, to protect Rudd (whose hadn't been). His mouthpiece was rinsed and crammed back in his mouth. His chin strap was yanked insultingly. "Fight him!"

He hated to leave the ropes, his middle was so tender. The bell alone was a stimulus to Rudd, who started lifting uppercuts immediately. But Kelly flared: the "Fight him" and his trapped imminence of being clobbered. The very ropes were wrapped in cloth a funeral black. He closed with Rudd and slugged, which was his natural fight and not the sharp-shooting boxing. He used long rights and overhands and long left hooks that packed their power at a distance where Rudd's shorter stuff would not.

It was a pleasure to his arms, and sweat flew off Rudd laughably wherever he got hit. He smacked him in the throat and made him gag, then had to move away in front of Rudd's slow, dragging charge. Moving meant he couldn't hold his range; either he missed or else Rudd grazed him. Rudd was a machine, with unvarying swings. All of a sudden Kelly shook him with a looping right which flattened the glove and, while the moment lasted, frenziedly swarmed him with close-quarter chops and hooks downstairs to disembowel him.

What Rudd returned to Kelly drove his stomach to his backbone. It collapsed him. He got more. He didn't count the punches. His legs would still work, compared to the rest of his body. Palsied, they carried him back, Rudd following and landing. Nothing hit belt-line like the first, but gloves blitzed into his face and chest. At each one Kelly's whole body shivered uncontrollably. He groped backward, trembly-legged. Rudd followed with the dragging gait. Kelly pushed out his arms to hold him off and fought the shakes and fought to clear his mind. *Jab! Jab him!* he started to remember, when he felt the ropes against his spine. He jabbed with both hands desperately, but Rudd plunged through and hit him on the lowest rib, hit him on the lungs and hit him on the liver. Kelly couldn't breathe. He was smothering with pain. His legs went trembling stiff; his head dropped forward. Rudd hit and knocked the mouthpiece out and nearly tore the hinging off the jaw. Kelly put his face into his palms and, half-unconscious, bent between Rudd's gloves. He couldn't move or hide or breathe. . . .

Rudd supported him against the ropes. Kelly clung around his shoulders, clumsy, coming to. With the action of actually helping and raising him, Rudd began slow-motion uppercuts, so as not to stall the round. A little while and Kelly crossed his arms and let Rudd use more force on them and fifteen seconds later was answering with tappings of his own. The middle minute passed in light and dream barragings of each other, perfect punches hard as pats. When Kelly put some bite in his, so did Rudd, and, Kelly having cleared his head, the fight resumed except Rudd remained outside of Kelly's jabs.

Kelly's mind and reflexes were functioning okay, recovering. The pain had numbed and wasn't hampering him. But, like a pro, Rudd watched the clock, and like a twenty-two-year-old, he couldn't bear to goof around the last few seconds. He plowed through Kelly's jabs and socked. Kelly was a bag of sand for him to lift. Lift him he did with belly punches and, like a sack being slit and emptied, Kelly sank away to shapelessness. The strength slid out of him like so much sand and he clung limply, slobbering on Rudd's shoulder. Rudd spanked his ass. The people clapped.

Crackers stripped off Kelly's stuff and Kelly fixed his eyes on him as if he were a doctor; he wanted to sit down but Crackers wouldn't let him. Crackers' face was screwed into the lines he wore when tending battered boys. "We yelled at him when he was lickin' you so bad, but you know how they never hear. He's worse, he's dumb." Kelly didn't try to speak. He wanted to lie down. Crackers kept examining him for cuts; he must be red. Finally Crackers shrugged and slipped from under him, so that he couldn't lean, and patted him and left him with a towel.

A towel. He focused on the fact of holding it, and touched his midriff gingerly and flinched. His eyes were fuzzed. In arena fights he'd taken maybe two or three beatings like this, when he was much younger. He groaned and was ashamed of groaning. He'd better not sit down; his body troubles would just harden on him. Actually his jaw was the sorest, but nobody minded a sore jaw as much. He walked a little bit. Two rounds in a gym—was it Rudd or was it him? Didn't matter, this was quits—he'd started coming again mostly to kill time; never again. A trainer and a fighter were arguing. What was there to argue about, how bad your organs were being rearranged? Kelly walked gently, not to let the pains harden.

A woman was in the gym, on spike heels, and stacked, and colored with an orange stripe up her hair. Kelly wondered if she belonged to Rudd, because he ought to have a good one. With any sort of a manager to move him he would move and Kelly might be telling grandkids of the day when he'd been walloped by a champ. Rudd's new partner was faring better. He was skinny, with ingratiating eyes, and was simply blocking punches, nothing else, and so he wasn't getting tagged. Oh, he'd feel for a chance to use his hook, which was his treasure obviously, but never more than started it. A trainer watched, placid and motionless, and next to him a peppy youngster bobbed and bounced, exercising, pumping his arms and simultaneously chattering gaily to the trainer, although the trainer gave no evidence of listening. The youngster's sweated hair poked wildly in all directions, while the trainer's stayed correctly combed. Kelly's middle grew more tender as the numbness lessened. Kelly would be like the trainer, not the youngster, from now on.

"Pretty tough boy, hey? Yeah, I wish I had him. Who doesn't?" Straws glanced over Kelly's frame for bruises. "Good experience for you to box him and you're lucky—anybody else'll seem easy. His manager says he will still let you box him and a little later he'll start paying you. You remember how he said he'd pay you?"

Kelly stared at Straws, unbelieving.

"You remember, don't you?" Straws chuckled nervously, patted Kelly. "Yesterday he said the last week he would pay you, son."

"You'll make me cry!" Kelly burst out. "You don't want to lose your lousy cheap three bucks you paid DeJesus! You're afraid to lose three bucks! You'd drop me afterwards and when you finished taking out expenses I couldn't buy a candy bar with what you left—and I'd be in the hospital!"

"You're a catcher, you're a bum!" Straws snarled and backed away as though from something vile and went to Crackers, thumbing at Kelly with a bitter-twisted mouth. Crackers gave no sign of a reaction, didn't even shrug. Straws went around to managers and thumbed. Some laughed at him for having gotten stung; some said so Kelly heard: "He don't like it, he don't work," and looked at Kelly bleakly. They had you if you still wanted to box, but Kelly didn't. He showered slowly, trying to sponge the pain away, slowly pulled on his civilian clothes, put his store teeth in his mouth—the crusher in his present mood—and sat caved in. He tried to talk to Peapod and his voice squeaked from the belting of the voicebox; his nose, swollen, hindered too. You had to go on living your whole life after you quit boxing. You couldn't be all busted up inside and sick and crippled because you'd taken extra punches when you'd got too old. A kid paraded to the mirror naked, a little jiggling nod of pride accompanying each step. It wasn't only stuck-up kids who jiggle-headed when they walked, but punchdrunks too; except a punchdrunk couldn't help it, and his face was molded grisly as a burlesque queen campaigner's, instead of, like the kid's, being snottily untouched—or else, like Rudd's, was mostly pad.

Kelly turned. China was pulling hairs out of his head to make a part with tweezers. It was awkward. He couldn't do it by himself and was embarrassed having Kelly see. Kelly was embarrassed too. China asked another Negro guy to help him. This one had a traced dab mustache, a knob of hair on his underlip, and Kelly felt so conscious of being white that he withdrew.

THE WITNESS

I HAD BEEN TRAINED AS A hospital technician in the army, and instead of the gleaming lab job uptown by which I had hoped to pay for graduate school, I was working in a defunct office building on the edge of the Lower East Side. It was a lab job, but what a lab! My cornflakes-and-cream face began to thin. I lived in a hair-raising rooming house, wondering what my BA was going to be worth and what would become of me. At the same time, however, life down there seemed bracingly rich. The pigeons of Venice wheeled over the roofs and the fountains of Rome spouted up from the hydrants. Churches in eight languages. You could buy diamondback terrapins and whole sheepskins, octopuses and sackfuls of beans. I still think somebody who lived near me could have traveled all over the world without seeing a face which really surprised him. The streets had the spicing of danger a young man likes—"Count Draculer" ruled in the block. Next door to my room was a death's-head guy who wept more than most people laugh. "My wife, my poor wife." I used to smile when we met on the stairs, being polite and supposing that he was laughing, until finally I distinguished the words. The family across the backyard kept roosters which woke me up in the morning.

Where I worked was a bleaker, Chicago-like district of factories, empty at night. It had been bustly about 1900 and was full of April-fool structures with gargoyles that goggled down. A fop stood on the edge of the roof of a perfume warehouse looking into an oval mirror. A large Christ close to him held a cross, and our wild-faced, collapsing building had MARY along its front in archaic lettering between wreaths of stone. My boss was a man named Darwin Hanes, forty-five. He wore a Purple

Heart pin, and ties that announced that he was probably a fruit. He was earnest, kind-natured, a flurrier at work, and rather the pure scientist in his intentions, except that he'd flunked out of medical school and dieted on nothing but personal bloody noses in the twenty years since. Anyway, he kept a room for projects of his own, with tubes of Tb and guinea pigs sneezing— we mopped down the floor with iodine. He was round-faced, pouch-eyed, and he made his acquaintances uncomfortable by staring at them for long, long stretches when he talked to them. Alone in the world, he was in that state seen commonly in New York where you give the person about five more years before he goes into a mental ward.

His cronies were Puerto Ricans, flattered to have an American friend. Darwin had learned Spanish during one of his self-improvement spates, and blew hot and cold on them, both sexually and just as chums. Hot and cold otherwise, he was touching answering the phone, full of belief and civilization and had a scientist's pride; then the choked pain in his voice (the doctors thought him a nut) when the man on the other end said he was sending a couple of patients over for tests and expected a kickback. He'd start shivering slightly, almost as though exhilarated. The world was all black, and, bastard of bastards, he'd make his way! If the girl in question came in with starched sleeves she preferred not to roll up for her blood test but took off the blouse instead, Darwin insisted on coughing until, despite my embarrassment, I pushed in to watch. He had a blackboard on which he did gene transposition equations, patterning himself on J. Robert Oppenheimer, perhaps. He'd put on a mystical stare and brush at the chalk on his hands absently, living the life of a genius as far as he could. He would come in in the morning having "seen the whole thing in front of me" just before falling to sleep, and would sit half the day at his desk muttering over the records he made of experiments, without much result—he'd "lost it."

A great man's life was variety, so he never stinted on phone calls or shopping around for equipment. He was interested in immense centrifuges, in the newest of sterilizers, and barrels of culture media. He believed busy men picked up the phone on the first ring—"Yes, yes, this is he"—taking notes on the margins of whatever was close. He had a soft voice that strung the salesmen along.

There wasn't much work, although enough not to pass the day reading, and I looked out on Lafayette Street a good deal, which was a large brutal one-way thoroughfare, always a drama in progress. At my window I got to be sort of a fixture. The drivers sped by, keeping up with the lights, and under the traffic's roar it was hard to distinguish other sounds, only the most frantic yells. More than once, happening to glance outside, I noticed everybody on the street had stopped and faced in our direction because of some appalling thing which had been going on underneath us for several minutes. A cross-section of business people came into the area, along with the garment workers, but the neighborhood acquired its peculiar tone from the bums wandering in from the Bowery a few blocks away. Though they were only a handful at a time, because of them nobody could ask for a drink of water at the soda fountain, get a car pushed, or ask any favor whatsoever. When the traffic light went kerflooey we must have had six or eight accidents before it was fixed, since everybody assumed someone else had called up about it. They were shoeless and bloodied bums, heaving, gasping and threshing bums. One never knew what might be wrong with them and never investigated. Once during the summer I remember a woman sat on the sidewalk from lunchtime on, apparently making different sounds. Several men stopped and peeked up her skirts but didn't do anything for her. A telephone company driver talked with her awhile from his truck; and a lady and a friend did busy themselves, except that they hurried on all the more hastily for their distress when three cabs refused to carry the woman anywhere.

It wasn't possible to watch, just as it wasn't possible for me to be very effective in helping without that becoming a full-time job. No one else did any more, not the priests or the nuns walking through, not the cops, though the cops did whatever eventually was done. The station house soon knew my voice as a crank's. It seemed I was running downstairs all the time—feeling pulses, dragging bums who passed out out of the road. I considered myself a kind of a last resort. The group at the gas station across from us would boot a man in the seat of the pants and bait him into "insulting" them so that they could grab their billy clubs, wrenches and tire tools and give him the run of his life. I shouted as loud as I could; I'd point from my window, establishing that I was witnessing it. Darwin never looked out, even when nothing was happening, and if he saw me hunch up from what I was watching, he left the room in a blaze of exasperation with the street and with savagery and with his own tender heart. He was sometimes hysterically harsh when he found a derelict trying to get warm in the hall but then was unhappy the rest of the day.

I was the laughing, skinny young man full of "minority" sympathy. I'd laughed at fraternity life, laughed at the army, and now in uncertainty I laughed at the city here, although it was the thinnest defense. In the bazaar-like streets around where I lived I began to flinch at the richness, not that it didn't delight me but because I was living amidst it too; nobody was going to come get me out. I had a girlfriend in the building named Ida with a preschool son and a husband long gone. We shopped from exotic market stalls or ate in great Chinese restaurants or went to the Statue of Liberty. She had nice black hair when she looked after it but malnourished skin—an eager vulnerable girl scalded as tough as a cat. Her eyes were marvelously brown and big, a very light, shining brown. We used to joke that she polished them, and, without contradicting the skepticism which had got knocked into them, they fluttered with accessibility. The lids constantly closed as if holding them in when I turned on my little charm, such as it was. Since she was the first person who'd ever been specially taken with it, I turned it on as hard as I could.

How she needed a man. She'd trot at my heels as close as a colt when we went down the stairs. She was a Japanese whorehouse in bed, and scornfully mocked me for being a mere boy, years younger than her, when her lopsided liking for me stuck out. She ate on eighty-five cents a day Welfare money with Tony, her son—powdered milk, pork hearts in government cans, and peanut butter. She fried powdered eggs and baked surplus flour. Forkfuls of butter and peas were a pleasure to her, and herring on crackers or a lamb chop was food for a queen. Her boy needed galoshes and toys and everything else and already worried about his mother. "Somebody" would give her a new pair of shoes, "somebody" would give her a sweater, he said, much too young to be hinting. He'd ask me to carry their garbage can down, and if I had change from an errand I'd done for Ida, he ran to her with it as if it were some kind of medicine.

She got colitis, bladder infections, aches in her ears, and every few days appeared to be out of her mind—she yelled in a hollow monotone. Her ovaries formed knots from nervous tension, and it was at one of these times that she thought she had gotten pregnant, which pulled us apart even as we pretended to join together. Fiendishly helpless, she was dependent on clinic interns and procedures whenever she or Tony got sick, and since the furnace broke down about once a week, this was often. At midnight Tony would suddenly wake up laboring to breathe, his temperature a hundred and two. A doctor or ambulance wouldn't be sent unless it went higher than that; and without my handouts she hadn't a cent for a taxi. One autumn night when I wasn't home she went into the street with Tony in convulsions in her arms, and found and convinced a patrolman that help should be called, afterwards standing beside him for twenty minutes. He was a young man and kept wanting to stop the police cars which passed. He went up on his toes, looking to see if the policemen were friends, but knew he would only be reprimanded for not having waited for the ambulance. In all these problems, the money I gave her was scarcely a starter because if her sanity really had cracked for as long as a couple of days, wheels would have been set into motion by the Welfare Department for taking her son away.

With each of us frightened, we sometimes had quite ecstatic excursions, as gay as one gets when the roof may fall in. We rolled the stroller along the East River at Delancey Street. The freighters that came sliding by seemed to fill it completely. We'd race them, while Tony hollered. I was fascinated by him. Week by week he was developing, and very much looking around for an older male. He watched me shave in the morning—"Is that how we do it?" He peered in when I took a shower and came up for regular "battles" with me. I grew very tender, toting him upstairs when Ida stayed late in my room and we put him to sleep on my couch. Then they spent the night, both in the bed. Such cooking, and dashing with tidbits for me—if she didn't claw me she gave me the moon. Once I had become a passion, she used every tool. She encouraged my fondness for Tony and told me he loved me, prompting trips up by him too to say that he did. The next time we were alone, he would say carefully, "I don't love you. Gene. I don't, you know." She thought me elegant, gentle and fine, and the security she needed so desperately came into it.

We went out at five in the afternoon, when the pigeon-fanciers were up on their roofs. White swoops and black shadow patterns. And every Friday a farmer sold tomatoes, comb honey, and cider and cheese in the storefront he rented—yellow cream, to make the sick well, and even cornflowers in the summer. He talked Ukrainian with his old neighbors, having left Ninth Street twenty-five years before. It was a link for him, and he was the man who'd made good on their block, and their tie to the woods and fields. He had flat farmer's arms, blue eyes, and a reprobate's face, the slack cheeks and lax mouth. "Just the pure stuff, nothing put in it," he said, like an article of faith, when we asked if the cider was sweet. His pear crates and his heavy old shirt and work boots were as good as a trip out of town.

Often we whooped out to Tompkins Park where there were the modern, sinuous slides. Dusk was the ideal time. Tony crawled through the whale-shaped pipes, giving out screams, and went up to the other children. He always seemed infinitely dearer than them. I followed as if he were mine. He'd negotiate some over a toy, then turn to me and throw his ball, or hike onto a higher slide, wheeing down with the tentative relish of someone enjoying what he knows is likely to be his chief recreation for the day. He always was interested to hear what we thought he'd particularly like to do next year, and he enjoyed these dusk go-rounds in much the same way that we did, for the magical sinking light and the teeming park emptied except for a few muted kids at the swings. He climbed the big slide with boosts from me—it was too high for him—and slid cautiously down. One afternoon they all had got hold of a pup tent and we helped put it up on the baseball field.

Tony had a luminousness, a resonance to him that was pitched very clear, a sing to his affections and words, perhaps just from growing up in a kind of state of emergency. After each bout with flu he seemed changed, a little bit older. He had awful dreams and toilet troubles and slept with his mother, but otherwise wasn't more nervous than plenty of children, so that whatever effect all of this would have was left in the air. Though he cried during Ida's lengthiest rages and spent many consecutive hours at the TV with that deadweight stare of a child, he remained promising. Of course Ida's hope was Tony in school, that there he would get the support he needed; some bright, cultivated teacher might take him in hand. He'd begun at a pilot-program nursery school and the teachers excited her with their comments. She and I had our ups and downs. My helping hand would be abruptly withdrawn, if only because she'd refuse it. In a day the world of dried Navy beans would return, the hard-as-nails mother. There was a middle-aged lesbian woman who paid Ida's phone bill and gave other aid in emergencies in exchange for the loan of the place certain mornings, and these visits increased. The plastering fell more frequently, provoking wilder reactions. The laundry piled up when the hot water failed and fifty cents wasn't forthcoming from me to take it around the corner. I wouldn't know what was happening downstairs, except that I'd hear a groan or two when I went past and resolved all the more to keep my distance, tired of catching sore throats from them, but worrying about the boy.

That Christmas: what a Christmas that was. No money, his mother bewailing into the phone. She'd determined to find some means of buying him a decent spread of presents but she had failed, and the failure knocked all her palisades down, the wolves howled—she was terrified about everything. We had had no contact for a couple of weeks, but the day before Christmas I overheard part of it and went down with a ten dollar bill for a tree and so forth.

"For who?"

"For Tony and us," I said, in the door.

"More games. More games and games and games," she told me in the most utterly exhausted tone, although already letting me rub her forehead. She rocked with it. "The dog act," she called it.

"You won't leave me alone. You won't stop knocking, will you? I must fill a function for you. I'm a pool you can splash in and see some results. You can see what a kick you have. You won't stop dropping in." Her skin shone with sweat and her eyes with exhaustion and her pale face looked flattened out. Soon she ran out of words and stood there, the uncleanable apartment in a shambles around her—a two-dollar strip of linoleum that was colored to look like a rug. "It's so painful when you just come and go. You don't stay, you don't say anything, you watch us and after a while you go again." But she gave up resisting and we rushed out and bought a bristly green tree and a bundle of presents, threw snowballs, and put on the radio for the carols, got benevolently drunk, and poor Tony had the kind of a day that he had much too often, a hectic heaped one which he was supposed to appreciate to the hilt, after the climax of weeping and tensions in which all the bones of the holiday had shown through—all the bones of the grownups' needs, of which his enjoyment was intended to be the relief.

She showed me she made up his bed like an adult's, since he was in school, and showed me a plant he'd been given and a drawing he'd drawn. She talked about getting a job once he was old enough, when she'd get off Welfare and burn all her rags. Rags they were too, a pitiful closet. I was brought up to date on everything, except hints were thrown out about new boyfriends in order to keep it all interesting. We talked through the weekend, Ida rooting for me wholeheartedly—my absurd boasts. Her mouth was like her accessible eyes, vulnerably wide, with a deep-set survivor's smile, a beautiful smile that probably owed part of its permanence simply to being such a large one. I loved looking at it while lying beside her, force-feeding her eyes. She was very acute but always the all or nothing type, and I was experimental. I had never been loved before and was somewhat the tyrant, or anyway fascinated by how variable women were, passion was so different from friendship. Her hair, if it wasn't limp, was lovely and springy. She had heavy long slick-skinned buttocks on rather short legs, and sharp breasts. I hung a bathtowel on myself to show how potent I'd gotten. She said she was glad we had met while she still had some of her youth left to give me. Her cheeks, as wide as a cat's, could be middle-aged sullen or wonderfully girlish. She had toil-ridden hands and a workhorse neck because she'd supported her family from the age of fifteen. She believed in the soothsaying stars as well as her dreams, the latter of which sometimes awed me. On the street, if I spotted her half a block down, she looked intimately linked to me like a relative, but all out of whack, preoccupied, miserable. She lived such a hair-trigger life that she'd wait half the night by her door for me to come home when we'd fought, yet be far from amenable. And I played her the dirty trick of connecting her in my mind with the maids my family had had in my early teens whom I'd never got up the nerve to try and lay but had wanted to. It was especially dirty since she was so conscious of caste. She'd had to leave school to scrub people's floors, and she would have hated me.

Darwin, meanwhile, was fizzing along. He concocted electrical devices as well as his medical stuff. He was the kind whom one feels the sorriest for, where the energy's there but amounts to nothing. He set a room aside for Ohm's Law, with shelves that almost met in the middle and equipment that hummed from the floor to the top. He began buying equipment in earnest, having inherited a few thousand dollars from an uncle who had died in Columbus, Ohio, and at once became secretive. This was the break that would bring the bonanza. Nights and Sundays he gave to the Law (Sundays his favorite day now), alone in the building except for the painters who had studios; and no love was lost among that bunch. Whenever you stayed in the building late you discovered new mysteries about the people. The fad was to buy camouflage cloth from the war surplus stores, so that, seen from the outside, the windows looked kooky and jungly.

The crazier a person was, the less tolerance he seemed to have for his neighbors, the less mercy or pity, and the harder he was to deal with. We had a woman we used to give leftovers to after lunch, but she wouldn't open the door no matter how loudly you called out her name. You had to put the food down, knock, and then leave, making plenty of noise so she'd know you were gone. Garbagecan Maisie. Darwin was called Quasimodo by the painters and, in turn, was raucous about their dead ends. He called me Lad, which, feeling as green as I did, I didn't mind. In his wilder states I was Androcles, never suspected of plots against him. He *was* quite like Quasimodo, in fact; once I had heard the name I couldn't forget it. He was cheerful and singing much of the time, blinking and deaf to the outer world. I could see him up in a belltower kicking and pushing away at the bells. His own plots were hair-raising, involving his tubes of Tb as they did. Of course he never carried them out but I had my first taste of powerlessness listening to him, because if I'd phoned the Health Department it was I, not he, who would have been judged to be nuts. With his animals, while he was humane in the short-term ways like water and food, his experiments grew very probing.

At my window, being left to myself, I went through a knightly period. If I saw a colored lady unsuccessfully trying to persuade a taxi to stop for her, I would go down and signal one and hold the door open, so that the driver wouldn't realize that I wasn't the passenger until it was too late. And a muscular, rebel Negro in a wheelchair lived around the corner. He would need to go out for food or a bottle of liquor, hating to ask a favor, and yet there was no other way to get over the curbs. When he was sober you'd see him swallow his pride and do it, but if he was drunk he would spin in his chair in circles for fifteen minutes on the edge of the traffic, yowling and sobbing, as the people avoided him all the more. So I used to go down for that.

Darwin took to working far into the night and bought a cot to sleep on at the office at midday. Either he slept scarcely at all or he slept like a dead man, wildly irregular. He cooked for himself and cooked for his mice, and the smells combined with the hammering from the locked room (he was putting up still other shelves) was crazy. As always when he was most withdrawn, he looked his most clean-cut and pleasant. He quit joshing with patients, worked in silence, and contaminated some of the culture plates in his haste. He had laughed at the neighborhood's burglar alarms, which were always going off, ringing all night, but now he installed one himself. The work we were given fell off. I spent long lunches watching the *bocce* on Houston Street, more Italian than Italy, really, or walked to the library or to one of the kosher sandwich emporiums or, in the summer, to the public pool near Avenue C where upwards of a thousand children would be swimming and the shrillness was universal like sunlight. Long lines waited behind the diving board: two lifeguards stood ready. Each kid climbed on and walked to the end, every step broadcasting that he hadn't the faintest idea about how to swim. In he'd plop. The guards took turns going in. Sometimes, leaving the lab at night, I passed by the local high school and found the whole street spread with trumpeters blowing away, the very bleakness everywhere else accentuating the gaiety. Postponing going home, I'd look through the paper for anything uptown to do. In the winter, if worse came to worst, I just sat in the subway where it was warm, reading the news with the men who dreaded going home to their wives. It was a year of intense wretchedness and happiness mixed, each deepening and giving the other color. On the subway, I amused myself by imagining that everyone sitting there was in armor of various sorts.

Ida's laugh became nearly as throaty when I kissed Tony as when I kissed her, since it was plain that I loved him a bit and that her hopes of marrying again weren't going to suffer because of her son. Her dependence made her even more of a hothead and made me take her for granted, besides. We avoided each other for days, despite his pathetic attempts to bring me back, when he'd knock at my door on his own initiative and tell me his mother wanted to see me, "needed" to (this after I'd heard her drunken yelling). But if we suddenly met, we'd get into each other's arms again, the sarcasms crackling, and her soft buttocks filling my hands. She'd lean her head back for a kiss. She compared her husband and me, both bastards, and laughed. "Has the dance palled?"—meaning her rivals. I'd never made so much love before, and found it was habit-forming. Success brought success. I chased, phoned, and dashed about, pushing, pushing defenses down, wet in the pants and wet in the mouth, this brimstone to her, naturally. The poor woman could hear the high heels through the ceiling if I brought someone in—I soon didn't. She'd upend her apartment and clean and explode, and the next day, hearing her yell at her son, I'd show up scared at her door for his sake, wondering who I should call. She asked who I was; had she met me before?

"You thump in here as if you're some king. Well you're not, you're just Johnny Average to me, and you better believe it. You're disgusting. You walk up and down those stairs—you're as arrogant as a turkey—I don't listen for you any more, you know. I'm not your biddy. You think he loves you. He doesn't love you. And I don't love you. I'm just curious to see what you'll come up with next. I learn, you know. I don't give a damn if a man like you drops dead in the street. You're just a fucker— yes, you're flattered, aren't you, you're such a boy. You think that's a good thing to be. You love me to kiss your chest. You think it's such a magnificent chest, don't you? You think it gives me a charge."

When she didn't drive me out, she clutched at me like a life ring, and didn't hear a word she said, because if I left she hadn't a clue as to why but would stand with the tears slowly penetrating the glaze in her eyes. Holding each other, we watched Captain Kangaroo, who was such a slob that he was a comfort. Tony, letting his oatmeal congeal, stared funnel-faced too. My notion was that, regardless of what happened between me and his mother, someday I would help to put him through college, or get him out to the country for summers. I hoisted him over my head, gulping down my delight in being a father; and the two of them lined up next to the door when I left for work to kiss me off.

Once she thought she was pregnant, everything was intensified. She talked about Tony for hours, as though lonelier now, bored with romancing, only the mother. The round-robin trading of sore-throat germs went on, like her crescendo-type suffering, standing past midnight behind the door. I felt horribly trapped. Why in god's name was I living down here? Half my attraction from her standpoint was because I came from another world. And why had I gotten myself in the fix—I'd forgotten how new the experience of winning love was. I'd made use of her and now it was nothing but castor-oil pains and a sanity stretched to its limits. I was scared to death. She with her neat, small ears, French nose, and her scrub-woman's lumpy arms— at my dreariest, I could imagine us going through the clinic mill and the intern's glances directed at me wondering why. The battered old tenement faucets rang like sleigh bells, and we were as merry as mourners, she sitting beside my knees. She hated men, worshipped men, and I rubbed her forehead, where the slamming she'd taken had registered most, the deprived and underdog bones. But she bloomed in exultancy, maneuvering her figure. She looked like a movie star. It was my baby. We were knitted together now. I was chilled to the bone! I'd never imagined such passion existed, much less that I might be the object of it.

When this aghast reaction of mine was clear, Ida got into more of a rage than anything else could have put her in. The luster went out of her skin. She turned into a fiery sick cat, bedraggled and humped. "Why didn't you let me alone? All right, we played house nicely and you found out you couldn't care less for the likes of me, I was beneath contempt; so why didn't you leave me alone? Why did you leave it up to me? It was so peaceful without you, I was getting along perfectly. But no, you wanted me on the string for the times when you hadn't anyone better. You revolt me, my friend. I don't want your baby. You figure out how to get rid of it. I haven't the energy to spare for you—I need what I have for my son." And, indeed, her efforts were all to shield him and keep up his routines.

Darwin puttered or pounded throughout the day in either his guinea pig room or his "juice" room, while Lafayette Street grew still grislier. Bums are straight out of a comic strip anyway, with their charcoal-smeared faces, their staccato-gapped teeth and gallows-bird postures that look like they've already been hung. When I watched a man chased down the street by a man with a knife, it was slapstick, like the comics, not TV realism. In the first place, the knife was outsized, and the man in front completely the wrong shape for running, and the man following him, though less bloated, ran like his feet were in boxes, plus the outlandish pursuers who were trying their best not to catch up. Real street fights were broken up into whirring fragments with baby-like *waaahs,* and bums fought with wood slats like Punch and Judy—the outcries, the shadow-show fury—till, after a long inaudible speech, the winner would take a few theater bows. My troubles at home didn't help remove me. On the contrary, I lost my perspective, I could see only the suffering. When I was pipetting something, I'd distinguish a child's shrieks under the rush of the cars and look out the window and see one being whipped on the legs for minutes on end by her father. What could you do? To step in directly would make it worse for the child—the mother already was doing her best to distract him—and to call the police would be more drastic yet, once the guy talked his way out of it and got the girl home. The only weapon was simply to watch—to *watch,* so that the fellow knew. Long after the family had left, I would be jumping up from my desk to lean out with cramps in my chest as if it were still going on.

In the army I'd worried about being "dehumanized," although in fact the army had softened me, but here was a vastly more brutal environment. The truck drivers shouted Giddyap at the bums pulling pushcarts. Even the street was caving in because some foundations had been misdug, and it threatened to block up the subway. I was just high enough to be out of throwing range if I shouted at people. When I was outside, myself, though, I quickly got expert at looking away. Either you watched pointedly or, for safety's sake, you looked away. One time a troop of housewives and I followed four or five friends who were beating the wife of one of them, stopping and pulling her into doorways, until our staring, our numbers, dislodged them.

Ida was shifting furniture to cause a miscarriage and doing hot baths. Going by on the stairs, I heard the brass ring to her voice, on the phone calling friends. After a minute she'd tap at my room to tell me the latest, since it was me in her body budding. Steaming with fear, she went up to Central Park and leapt off the boulders. My hair stood stiff to hear about it. I hugged her, begged, and yet finally had nothing to say, realizing how little the difference was between jumping off boulders and going to the doctors that Darwin knew. She was petrified; she said that her life was a wreckage; she felt hot to the hand as if she were running a temperature and could hardly put two words together, afraid that they might take Tony away, and frightening the daylights out of me. All of a sudden, however, worried that it was some cruel piece of egotism, I would look at her and be tremendously pleased at the pregnancy, sexually excited, and go over her with my hands. She felt the same way immediately. We made the most tender, delicious love, with her stomach the center of it, never so sexy.

Darwin considered me some sort of link to the rest of the world, and joked about "raping girls" and other misconstrued

normalcies, though disarmingly gentle about it. He told World
War II stories, sitting across from me at his aluminum table and
wiping his ribs with a towel if he wore no shirt. He liked to keep
to a schedule, to overwork, which wasn't easy in a lab such as ours,
and occasionally to take time off for an indulgent talk with me.

"I'll tell you, lead your own life. Nobody has any business
with you. They won't understand what you want to do. They'll
laugh at you out of ignorance. So you don't ask permission from
anybody when you pick out something you want to do, you just
go ahead, and then you won't have any problems," he said, the
brief phrases to add pithiness. But this successful man's manner
was rendered incongruous by the misfit's tone, the schoolboy
solemnity he gave everything. It was in his mouse room that he
could seem to be bluff the most briskly. The hundreds of
rustling creatures did seem like employees—another twill factory in operation. He inspected them with overseeing interest,
or picking them up, injected their stomachs, their poor little
pots, with that undeniable affection which experimenters,
seeing them always as plural, have for their animals as a group.

Our peppiest moments came when a bold bum would
wander in wanting his heart listened to. Darwin got shouty, but
if the guy didn't run out of the office or wasn't insulted he
usually would change around. He wrapped his stethoscope
affably into his hand like the doctor he'd wanted to be. He'd sit
on the edge of the desk and chat like a boy with a younger boy,
wreathed in smiles, not so puffy-faced now. These were his
cheeriest periods of all, as if he realized that he could still be a
part of the world. The bum inevitably blossomed out too,
thought he was awfully skillful to get so much free attention—
blood pressure taken—and even forgot his worries about his
health. The loudest voices are the voices of bums. The final
survival energies, drawn if necessary from everywhere else, seem
to go to their throats. We had several memorable specimens,
stuffed into their clothes like badly made puppets, the clothes

brown and gray and all torn—stains, a scrap of a beard. They were bodiless heads. They were so badly off the only reason they still could walk was that they had wasted away to nothing. But the voice mushroomed, as strange as the lush, unnatural plants which grow out of dead things. Or sometimes the only piece left of a bum was his laugh:

"Wherever I happen to be I'll come in for a checkup every few months, just to be on the safe side. I'll look-see if I can't see a fairly intelligent-looking doctor some place pretty close around. I don't like to walk too far away for it. That way you don't have to worry, you know nothing is sneaking up on you, and if you do what the fellow tells you to do you're gonna be okay until the next time—little heart murmur or something, it's gonna be all right. Oh I can take the cold, I'm very good on that. I know the techniques. They trained us with that. I was up on the DEW Line three years you know. I was up in the Arctic. A lot of these bums wouldn't last a day. Three years of that and you'll take the cold fine; you can take anything. Yeah, you'll see some snow up there, you'll see some dandy cold."

He was like a boy who was shining shoes, this one, with his pert line of gab and the patronizing smiles we gave him. He had hands like a turtle's skin, and strips of newspaper inside his socks, a red toucan nose, a white and red face like a ham bone, and he shook like a soaked sourdough from his illnesses. His ragged coat flapped in the wind like a flag when we watched him leave. Right away he begged from a car at the light, not to lose the boost to his confidence: he put his hands carefully behind him and stooped like a bon vivant to speak to the driver.

We also watched the fences at the garage. I laughed but Darwin was bitter like any respectable citizen under siege. It was hard to tell what was going on because they also worked at regular mechanical jobs. They filled up the station with cars and sweated all day, with a reputation for piddling cheating. But then these cryptic vans would pull in, *Pong's Produce, Old*

Reliable Pipe and Joint—ten-year-old trucks which had been painted over a dozen times. They'd move the whole garageful in order to stick the truck in the back, getting very excited and busy.

There is nothing likeable about criminals. They're sneering creatures, ready to turn vicious in an instant, and it was an exacerbation to have them placed opposite us. Of course it made little difference to them when I waggled my finger. They'd grab up tire irons and chase a man. If a Negro drove in for gas, they gave him a Queen Isabella bow and had him wait, pretending to be just about to come, in order to see how long they could keep him. "You goddam bow-and-arrow, get outa here!" They worked, they threatened, in absolute incoherence—a shrug, a lunge at the breastbone. They couldn't talk without jabbing their hands at the person, the mark of respect being not quite to touch him. My stomach got turgid and hot as I'd watch an incident develop. For some reason I went back to the screw-you signal of my boyhood and pointed with that, trying to make myself heard. I shook in confusion for the next half hour whether I'd stayed to watch the scene out or whether I'd ducked away like Darwin. They robbed their own pay phone when they needed change, and the Puerto Ricans hated them too and used to write "warps," "gunnies," on the wall at night after the place closed. One Sunday Darwin watched a car which they hadn't been able to fit inside completely stripped, down to the axles, by three Negroes. He was delighted. It yawned there Monday, while the men fumed.

The four were related, I got the impression, except for a muscle-bound fellow who seemed the most decent. The dominant guy was a blast of straight vigor. He worked a twelve-hour day in his shirt sleeves into December, never ceasing to bluster and shout. He ate with his left hand and worked with his right, talking over his shoulder to the hired, muscle-bound one and yelling ahead to his fat husky brother. The brother, with an unpleasant face, kept up with his share of the jobs but sourly. He had the children who played nearby, attractive twins. The fourth man, who was maybe a cousin, was nervous-natured and thin and tall. He had lithe, precise hips that pumped when he walked. He was the most unpredictable and independent and had an oddly chic wife who came and sat in their car every few days while he worked. She looked nice; she was a softening influence, very much gentling him. A snide scowl snuck over him when he got the snow shovel and ran for a bum (they'd let the guy go in a corner and start to pee first). The two children did not have a dampening effect, but when his wife was around none of this happened. He resented me—he was the one who stared back. If I passed on the street he usually quit working sarcastically, though we never spoke.

Virgil Grissom and Hubert Humphrey were driven through on their way up from City Hall. We had a vegetable wagon clatter by daily that serviced the luncheonette downstairs. I looked down at the part in the horse's mane. The Hoodoos fought with the Roman Emperors in the next block. And we had Light and Gas men. They were trying to pump out a manhole before doing some job, except that it filled up again every night. In the morning they strung tapes around the hole, hung warning flags, and set the pump going, and smoked and Coked the day away until the last hour, when they took everything down again. And a mailman made constant pickups—it has to be seen to be believed how many are made.

By the garage was a liquor store owned by a man with a villainous voice and a face shaped like smoke, gray as smoke, who flapped one hand smartly behind when he zipped along on a delivery. He parked in the station and was friends with the bunch, although he considered himself a cut above them. Ours was the civilized side of the street. Right below me was a classical tailor, who suffered like a sunfish in a pail; and, next door to him, a womanly printer whose window display had not been changed for fifteen years and whose mouth was as large as his stomach, the better to laugh with, presumably. He cut the ads for his son-in-law's business out of the paper and carried them around like snapshots. Then his cobbler friend, as skeptical and as seamed as a jockey. He hammered so neatly it was like a stage set: stroke, stroke, the sole was fast; and the nails in his mouth for comic relief. He had a comedian's mouth anyway, and he'd go out and pet the vegetable horse. Two Puerto Ricans ran the luncheonette in eager immigrant fashion. The best thing about them was how they walked off at six o'clock, rolling like seamen, relaxing so hard. They were agreeable and got along fine until the slap-dash cooking cut into their business. They responded by cooking more hastily still and by stinginess with the portions and reducing the menu, so that it was another sad story.

We had plenty of people around and yet we had nobody. When something happened and I would go down I would be on an empty street. In my way, I was expert at preserving my own skin. I never "closed" with anyone, just put myself close at hand. When a car jerked out of the traffic one time with screams from inside, I opened the door on the girlfriend's side to help her get out, not the man's, and retreated as he came after me. "Oh you better run—he'll kill you!" she shrieked. I could see Darwin's pale face above me, and the jockey squinted behind his window as if he were watching a dangerous jump. Darwin believed he had a sixth sense, which made him especially fearful. By now he was sure I'd get clobbered. He told oodles of war stories, remembering more as he went along, and displayed the scars of a beating he had received from some young homosexuals in an earlier phase. They'd tattooed the star on his hand, which alone would have made it impossible for him to return to a more normal life, he claimed. Breakdowns and other new chapters were revealed. An old anxiety about robberies returned. He stopped inviting his Spanish friends up because they might see the equipment and be tempted. He checked the door to the roof twice a day. "That's where they come, off the roof." While he was scared to sleep in the lab, he was even more afraid to leave it unguarded. He used army phrases, shaking his head and gritting his teeth. He even quit leaving our leftovers outside the old lady's door down the hall in case she broke in some night after more.

But he was for *me,* telling me twenty times that he would be my character witness. It was often the police I was battling. In civilian clothes a guy would march off a vagrant, refusing to show him his badge, just whacks. Or when they stormed in in response to a call, arrowing down Lafayette the wrong way, these were the large, lengthy scenes, spreading across the wide street, repetitious but excruciating after you had seen a few. The gold-badges slapped with open hands, as a detective would. The silver-badges poked their clubs like bayonets until a pretext came for swinging down. I bought a camera and drafted letters to the *New York Times.* I fretted on the outskirts, trying to copy cap numbers, and more than once I only saved myself from being arrested by backing off. The standard ending became to find myself being forced to lay my ID cards across the roof of a police car while all the stuff was written down, to stand there, hands on top of the car, in front of the open door—it functions as a sort of station house—until the decision was made as to whether to arrest me, too, or not.

I got nutty, no question about it—more compelled and susceptible, quick to tear and quick to tremble. My eyes had been rubbed raw. The fire escapes on the garment factories filled up with people if a Negro was involved, and some of them would rush downstairs and fuss alongside me on the edge of the action. My ragged nerves were like theirs. I had seen so much violence by now, so many atrocious injustices, that any beginning carried its whole plain progression for me—I understood Darwin's sixth sense. The police were the same, for that matter, and so were the gas station toughs. Everybody picked up from the last time. Anger from then, or anguish, whatever it was, piled onto the new occasion. In a flash the despair poured back, and I would be leaning over the patrol car hood again, my teeth practically chattering.

"No, no sir, buddy, you take out your fucking license yourself! I don't handle nobody's wallet!"

It was December, that awful Christmas, and we had the procession of Santa Clauses coming out of the subway all day with their locked boxes and Santa Claus bells. Their terminus was a mission nearby on Houston, so we had the entire city's street Santas, who were really just ordinary bums dressed up in red and white, limping along much as usual—they didn't bother with stomachs for them. We also had Fire Department exercises going on within a couple of blocks. I needed a vacation badly, needed to get to the country; I was irritated simply by humans and human activity by this time. If a bus driver reached the end of his route and wanted to turn around, I argued with him. The signs on a church or a synagogue that said that it closed at 8 p.m. stuck me as pharisaism. At my cheerfulest I typed myself with the bearded, anachronist Jews in shiny black coats, only a very few left, who still hauled their pushcarts through all this madness in the old style, purple with sweat, having no relation whatever to it.

Though the frog tests I did on Ida continued to run negative, she wouldn't menstruate and the doctor thought that he felt a pregnancy rather than cancer—he said it was *something*. I would drop in on the way to work, if possible, because of my own shakiness, instead of at night when I would have to stay longer. I gave her money and horrified hugs and pained, gingerly looks which tried to convey affection. It's hard to reconstruct exactly what she was feeling since I was trying to avoid being aware of it. She "suspected" I didn't love her, though of course I believed I had never pretended to; and she really thought a good deal of the time that she was going to die or at least be made sterile. She dreamt of water, of babies, of me, of death, and raged against being a woman, while at the same time she was trying to shield me from what she was going through, that is, except for the nights when she heaped her sufferings on me in blinding half-hour explosions, her voice like a flatted cornet. She ate and threw up as if she were pregnant, and looked taut and scrawny with that violin-string attenuation of a cat which drags itself. Then, next morning, what a Liz Taylor opened the door, belly-ing gay as the clouds! I'd bite her. I had a permanent cold from exhaustion.

Her room and a half had her marriage furniture in it, appropriately mismatched and in faded bright mummy-like colors. When there wasn't another reason, my heart went out to her for the apartment alone, so unspeakably dismal and small, and she without even the subway fare to get out. The layers of paint and linoleum extruded dirt from tenancies fifty years past. The two beds took most of the space. The books were her husband's Genet, the decorations her own sporadic attempts which she couldn't get rid of when the mood left until she saved enough money to buy something else. I regarded the place as mine for loafing ("your doll house," she said), and we still had rather happy, whimsical evenings sometimes, with billing and cooing, no barbarities. We lived on three different planes, mine being the mundane. Ida was in a shadow world, smelling life, smelling death, the surface realities scarcely a glimmer part of the time. She drew upon every ounce of her concentration to manage the details of Tony's existence, yet he chirped out the window obliviously. He had the most marvelous shrieks and chirps, like nothing I'd ever heard before. I almost wanted the baby born. He shot with his gun out the window too much and chased the cat hard, had very pitiful moments, but mostly one wondered whether he wasn't living on borrowed time, whether such glee in defiance of logic and of his surroundings wasn't going to have to be paid for. Certainly in other respects he could go either way. He was slummy-faced, coarse and tough for a while, as if growing up to be somebody I wouldn't be able to care about. Then in the afternoon, maybe, his eyes would spread open, his face would go soft, as he listened to one of his mother's tales of Aesop. He was precociously gentle whenever she reached her rope's end, just as Ida after an incendiary couple of hours always stopped short and knelt down in order to make it up to him with an effusion of playful intuitive love.

Twice the social worker dropped by unannounced for what was called a Complete Drawer Count. And the tenement pipes rang like railroad bells. "Just hold onto me," she'd whisper, as crazy as eels. It was *"Please* don't stare!" or else "You're not looking at me!" when I was too anxious and pitying. The truth, as we waited for word from the doctor to act on, was that the danger that she'd have a breakdown was worse than the risk of any abortion. She was Catholic, and I rubbed her resisting back by the hour while she talked. I was a futile substitute, but she was afraid she'd lose Tony if she went to a priest, and she made me afraid to go to one too. Listening, I couldn't fix on a plan for any of the eventualities. There were other shouts in the building but not pitched like hers, and she lay with her head in my lap, so that I saw the tears in her nose and the swollen blood vessels. Tony writhed on the floor.

"I've taken so much and what have I got to show for it? I have you here, younger than me, almost a child really, because you were hard up, and now you like to think of yourself as wonderfully kind and honorable. I don't care who's with me. I don't even know where I am. Have you ever felt neuter? Well that's how I feel. I don't feel like a man and I don't feel like a woman. I'm dead, I'm an idiot, I don't feel. I wish I were a tree, or have I read that somewhere? I must have. Nothing is original with me, is it? I don't believe in God but I'm afraid of Him. I don't particularly like you, but I loved you—that's not original either. I don't want to sleep with any more men or have any more babies but I don't want to be sterile. I see horrible figures in dreams, but they're the best company I have except for my son. I'd do anything not to die, but I want to die."

Just as dreaming of having a breakdown is said to tap off the pressure building towards one, when the janitor in our building cracked up Ida appeared to revive, to catch a kind of a second wind. It was a hectic long night. The guy was afraid his relatives were going to kill him and begged for help in heart-rending yells, but he was the one who was armed and they were only afraid for their lives. He ran into the tenants' rooms for protection, and when we ran out, he followed, afraid to be left by himself. With his knives in his hands, he went down on his knees and begged us to spare him.

Soon we were to find out she wasn't pregnant at all, but I'd sunk into a state where my laughing and joking were of no use. I couldn't eat. I was worn out, bewildered and worthless as far as assisting her was concerned, and unable to pick myself up or take a sensible trip or take some good pills. There had been no chance to collect my wits and hunt uptown for a job. I thought I'd never get out of this, and the winter shut most people indoors, so that the suffering seemed that much worse. If you dodged past a barefoot beggar, the blood on his face had froze. The old Jews took temporary respites, but the bum pushcart pullers continued wretchedly. Many drivers hardly acknowledged their right to the street anymore, so long after the heyday of pushcarts.

It may have been an impatient attempt to scare the man or a misjudgment because of the novelty. Maybe the cart didn't register on the truckdriver's eyes, being neither a pedestrian nor a motor vehicle. Barreling along and simply not seeing it, he clipped the cart from the rear, spinning the man in front of him. He didn't begin to brake or swerve until it was done.

We called the police from upstairs. Darwin had bought some goldfish and was tinkering with the aeration. By now it was established he never was going to go down on the street if something was happening; and I didn't object; I didn't want to go either. But I'd seen the accident. The man was lying there with nobody touching him, and I still had a sense of being "medical": in fact appeals on those grounds were occasionally made to our window from down on the street.

He looked dead from close up. I asked in the liquor store if we oughtn't to phone for an ambulance. The fellow was doing paperwork.

"Nobody can call an ambulance except the cops. You know that. What's the matter with him?

"He was hit by a car," I said. I'd disliked his preposterously sinister face for so long; he turned round and grinned.

"Yeah? Well probably you ought to call the cops, don't you think?"

I was unable to answer that. Outside, I looked up and saw Darwin worrying in the window, as were the printer and the two Puerto Ricans on our side of the street, although they had no apparent reason for worrying about me. A nervous tick in my cheek asserted itself; I realized I was bone-tired.

"Phone for an ambulance," I yelled to Darwin. The victim appeared quite decidedly dead, however. For all the illness I'd seen, he was my first dead man, and yet since he looked like hundreds of magazine pictures—the ragged refugee dead by the road—the sight could not have been more familiar. Every night going home I went by at least one drunk passed out, usually in danger of freezing. Dead as they looked, I went by assuming, like everyone, that somebody else was going to stop, because to see to them would have tacked on an hour or more to my day. This was absolutely routine, but I felt for a pulse with a sadness that had a momentum behind it—he *was* dead, I knew. Sick, shaky, I wanted to laugh. The pity I had withheld so many times had caught up with me.

The traffic streamed by. A couple of the gas station men came out to wave it on so that their entrance wouldn't be blocked, and the truckdriver passed cigarillos around. He was very upset, an outspoken, balding person in a checked wool jacket. It was after four, nearly dusk.

"They shouldn't be let on a street like this. I mean it's for stuff that's going through, you're supposed to go around twenty-five, thirty-five miles an hour. Poor baby. That never happened to me before. Right out of the blue, they step in front of you and you've killed somebody. Poor bastard. Jesus." He walked around between us. I didn't nod to agree but, on the other hand, didn't find him objectionable. The difficulty was that I had an exact image of what I had seen. As crisp as a diagram, the truck had traveled in a straight line. The cart had been in the path of that line and at no time had the truck hesitated. The impact with the man was too searing to bring to the front of my mind but it was indelibly there. The daylight, dim to begin with, was rapidly vanishing.

I went up to the lab, since I could feel myself get incoherent. The man was dead; no sense in gawking about. "Oh, all bashed to hell, that's all," I told Darwin. "Hit him from behind." The truck had *McMartin's Scotch Whiskey* on it and a pasteboard bottle, and the driver, we saw, walked into the liquor store and provoked enough interest that the proprietor at least poked his head out the door. The Texaco bunch toed the cart frame. "Vamose," they said to a carload of Spanish, keeping the driveway clear.

From the gestures, a consensus was forming by which the pushcart man was to blame. Nobody checked him again, and I wondered if I hadn't been too quick in presuming him dead. Though this was nonsense, I came down. They were by the truck, looking for damage. Without much basis, I got the idea the guy might have handed out a few bottles as I was coming downstairs. The cart man, in Raggedy-Ann clothing, was partly thrown on his side, with his head bloodied and his seat all cut up from a bottle of wine that had been in his back pocket. Amazed, I recognized him as the one who had sat and chattered to us about the DEW Line in such an incongruously lively way. All of that spunk and spark smashed up like a broken doll—it revolted me.

"They shouldn't let them out on the street, or you'll even see them up on the sidewalk. No light on him, no way to see him," the driver complained. The others wanted to drag the cart over a bit to let the traffic pass by faster. "Leave it. It's way the hell out there," he said. But with a scared, guilty face like mine might have been, he swung back to me as if I was the one he wanted to convince because I was next to the body.

"Nevertheless he *was* on the street," I said.

"Nevertheless?" He sounded the word, mixing respect and sarcasm. "What are you, a doctor?"

"No he's not a doctor, he's just a Nosy," chuckled the thin mechanic. I'd always been glad it wasn't one of his huskier partners who had taken the special dislike to me, but I saw he could beat me up easily.

"I knew him a little," I said.

"You knew him?" Bolder, the driver asked with his eyebrows *why* I knew him. I hunched by the body, feeling righteous and safe. After walking off, he came back and stared down at the man in sad disapproval. He leaned with a nervous snort, touched the man's rear, and smelled the alcohol on his finger. "Maybe the noise frightened him." His hands did the noise, then the cart veering into the traffic suddenly. Charades over drunks were so commonplace, one had to remind oneself that this fellow was dead; and—although I was glancing for suspicious bulges on them—the way the garage crew was looking at me, I might have been the man who had run the bum down.

"I knew him. Yeah," the store owner said, leaving his door-way. "All the bums around here." He puckered his mouth, looking down, as if to convict any customer of his. The driver asked who delivered his liquor to him.

Why was I being so punctilious, I wondered? I'd sympathized with the driver at first—why get him in serious trouble when nothing constructive would come of it? The man would be just as dead. In the same way as the gas station bunch had taken his side partly to spite me, wasn't my attitude the reverse? With their long-flanked red faces and their choo-choo-choo vigor, I'd never seen them so close before. It was like bars being removed. Here they were next to me, no barriers. And they all had the camaraderie of living in Queens and shaking their heads at the neighborhood. The dynamic, blocky, all-vigor guy kept leaving to heave himself onto the fender of the *Pong's Produce* truck and practically disappear inside its motor. "You live in that place?" he asked me, pointing.

"I work there."

"You work there?" He laughed at the building facade with its blotchy camouflage curtains and the wreaths around MARY.

"I'm a medical laboratory technician," I said, trying to invoke the immunity more than the prestige.

"Where do you live?"

They listened, these people I had been pointing at, judging and needling for months. It was too late to leave and I saw that by staying here to argue this issue I had lost whatever effec-tiveness I had been having up in my window. It was like the police interrogation would be. When they heard where I lived they guffawed.

The cart had carried junk cardboard, ground almost to powder by the traffic by now, and pedestrians pumped past as thick as the cars. By standing still I got the sensation of manag-ing some kind of a show. The most touching detail was a handful of wooden letters the size of a child's blocks, O's and

H's, which were strewn alongside the gutter. In warm weather the cart must have been used as a hot dog wagon.

"Tell me something. Why are you all the time sticking your hand out the window? Are you trying to make a U-turn?"

We all laughed. The all-vigor fellow pushed up on his arms from the *Pong's Produce* motor to hear it repeated. A postman in a truck made a pickup, dragging his sack past the body. Infuriated that I was trembling, I searched for the top of the bottle, thinking that if the seal was still on I might prove the man had been sober. The early darkness was very confusing.

Once the cops came it was the trial in advance, acquittal quickly a certainty. They copied the license number on the tail of the cart. They shared with the gas station people that extraordinary beefiness found in the city. The owner of the liquor store emerged to touch the victim's rear end and convey the idea that he had been drinking, and the expression on the dead bum was no help. Besides being so very surprised-looking, he looked haughty and quarrelsome compared to when he had chattered to us about Hudson's Bay. It was the face of a man with freezing wet feet, with scarlet, goose-pimpled hands and neck, who was trying to ignore the shouts from the traffic and ignore his misery. When I drew my mind back to those moments before he'd been hit, I remembered no drunken appearance. He'd pulled like a dutiful, suffering horse that knows that its work is the lesser of evils. Now he looked like a crunched guttermouse made up for the role of a bum, with the stubble and stock ruby nose.

"Old bums like that, they don't carry a light, can't hardly control what they're pulling, and they turn their ankle or they slip where it's wet—had a little too much—and out he goes in the lane. It's a crime when they're out like that," said the thinner garage man.

"Actually, the light was pretty good then," I argued in a despairing tone to the police. "I work right across the street, and he was coming down very fast, right by the curb. The poor guy was right in front of him. I don't think he ever did see him. It was much lighter than this, plenty of light. He didn't have his headlights on, himself, as a matter of fact, so it doesn't make any difference if the cart had a light of its own because it wasn't dark enough yet to need one."

Hoots from the witnesses. The scorch-faced owner of the liquor store said, "No, he had a load on."

The driver glanced over to where he was parked. "Well I turned 'em off, naturally, but I had 'em on, they were on."

"Sure, his lights were on."

I was chilled by the gas station group, for whom until now I had been pretty much of an abstraction, up in an upper story. They were giving me total attention. The stream of Santas climbed out of the subway, limping by us, and the ambulance came; another mail pickup was made. When the body was gone it required an effort to remember there even had been a body. As in the rehearsal, when they talked to me the police turned to look at my building. With their faces trained neutral, they asked how I'd seen through the camouflage cloth.

"I'm a medical laboratory assistant. We don't have that. We have the sign about blood tests in the window."

My home address registered badly again, as it would have in court, and perhaps I hammered too hard at the light being so good. Also, their first impression of me was marked by my searching look as to whether we'd crossed swords before, a look which must often betray petty criminals—that and the way I dropped my head like an exhausted bull in the ring, very small, windedly quivering. The uniform looked different to me. That charcoal blue—business blue. It had become almost impossible for me to talk to police without being hostile or supercilious, and so it was like a job interview, where my name was being written down but I knew I would never be hired.

I left work right afterwards, in a tumultuous funk. The killing, the codger gabbing away happily in our office only the week before, and everybody's closing over the facts of the accident—I felt as if I had flu. Darwin seemed queer as a coot with his star on his hand and his goldfish and mice and heavyweight name, and I wanted out.

As I crossed the Lower East Side, the record stores blared, the peddlers' trucks jingled, mocking me with a storm of sounds. A priest in an overcoat walked up and down on Elizabeth Street, since he hadn't a cloister, holding a flashlight over his breviary and whispering the words. Kids were clouting a ball. They towered it up seven floors, then tried to spot it before it fell. A cat was making love to a dog. The light was so mutedly rich in night colors that my eyes led a life of their own. The vivid neons had a handmade gleam more stimulating than neons uptown, and the squint I'd developed, the squint of a person who couldn't walk five or six blocks without seeing a man slugged, an arrest or a beggar, widened out in spite of itself. My eyes crowed. I heard Hindi, Rumanian, Cantonese, Polish, each lilty. A guy was thocking an oud with a spoon. Two beatniks had hung a piece of cardboard on their fire escape to communicate with the girl opposite—"Hey, Sweet!" Children spilled whooping across the sidewalk, and the off-Broadway theaters seemed like opera houses up in the Yukon, dowdy, primitive structures, newly white-washed, in the midst of a wilderness boom.

In my block the bookie's bird store had become bona fide. His life's enthusiasm was these evenings, when he really sold birds and sunflower seeds. He sat on a bin in his pigeon coop engulfed in wings, while he talked through the wire to a couple of pals. The whole block was dream-like and misty, the light Parisian, with every building a different color and height and shape, the fire escapes zigzags of rusted orange, and the rooftops running along in a dum-de-dum-dum. Now I was squinting against the beauty—I must not be strong enough to live here. I caught a glimpse of two fencers upstairs in a loft, and a man inside a locked girdle store was playing his fiddle to a macaw. I looked at the lemons in the street stalls, at the mounded-up oysters and booties and Preen, feeling utterly flattened. That Ida's future should depend upon what I might choose to do was the worst circumstance of all.

She was plenty crazy at first that night: acute concentration on me. Her squeeze when we hugged was too strong to have any meaning as such and had none of the sexiness that was best at arousing concern.

"Something happened?" she asked. She was stroking my back to loosen it. With her harrowed face, which was so much more anxious on my behalf than anyone else's would have been, she looked at me with an open love that overwhelmed me in shame, that she should be sorry for me, tenderly reading my muscles for tension, after the way I had dodged in and out the last weeks. A large face, like a boy's from medium range, like a woman's if you were close or away several yards. Brown eyes, black sweaty hair, and that great wide survivor's smile of hers, as serene as a smile in death. I got a fresh sight of this gritty girl who thought she was carrying a child by me and who was living on powdered eggs and charity clothes and plain lonely terrified misery. I realized how little I'd done, how execrable it would look to me in a few years if I hadn't shut out the memory altogether. My god, how little I'd given her! Beer to help her relax at night? Not usually, unless we were necking. Blueberries, avocado, if I was having them? No, not unless we were eating together. A forkful of buttered string beans would have given her pleasure sometimes. I must have been mad—her son standing between my knees looked at least twice his age because of the life they were leading—I'd lost perspective completely!

I ran out and got mushrooms, steak and oregano and so on, and spoiled the meal only by hardly talking. Tony wanted the fathering element of it in equal proportion with the food, so he sat on my lap to eat, which he did with politeness and dignity. It was a funny meal. My affection for him gushed up until I could scarcely swallow, watching his every move, and with Ida I was the penitent husband. I'd forgot how at home we could be, although she assumed my silence was because of her pregnancy. But her glance lost its glaze; she got peaceful and sweet. She drew the big circles under my eyes with her finger.

"You've had a worse time, haven't you? You've worried more. You're very generous. Yes, you are," she said when I shook my head. "And I'm not after you, you know, that's not what I want, you mustn't feel any pressure like that." At her simplest and most attractive, she went on about how nice I'd been. She meant it, but at the same time I was thinking that we were half married already, and how fine it was to have supper this way, that to go through the further formalities might be right for me too. Once she was given a little stability, there would be just her warmth, no jaggedness. I couldn't bear picturing the boy dragged off to an orphanage, and felt protectively head-of-the-house. I began reaching under the table, and told her the accident story, more detached about it than I would have imagined an hour before. We hurried the dishes, mouth to the sweater already, and got Tony to sleep. She was a bit gaspier than I liked but very giving. Small breasts with large nipples, and an overall skinny toughness I loved—geisha-small feet with high arches, a mouth like a plum. It was another night when the loops bound around us made us relish each other all the more.

The next day we found out the loops didn't exist. I stayed home from work to get over the pushcart episode and she came in at noon from the doctor's and said he had made up his mind it was a false pregnancy. The explanation was skimpy because we had paid out so much already she didn't pay to have a long conference; but we scarcely hugged once after that. I left the house in blank angry relief and didn't go near her apartment for almost two weeks. I sought out a Negro girl I'd been flirting with, to enter that brittle, tight little set, the dark half of which wanted to go up in the world and the white half of which wanted to go down. Since I, of course, wanted to go up like the Negroes, I didn't quite fit at the parties. She was the life and direction at them. She was impatient, tense, prickly, a virtuoso with people. We had one banner day, plus three club-foot attempts to repeat.

The district absorbed me all over again. I wandered as I hadn't since first arriving. Moist, late December weather with wind and sun, when winter hovered just overhead, giving one more day's grace, now another. I got the exuberant sense that here in one spot was my whole fellow family of man. The racial mix on the streets brought a racial peace which was affecting if you went into other parts of the city. For both colors the process was rather like learning to fly—so many thousands of hours of looking to be put in—and down here we'd gotten farther along. Avenue C had a small-town flavor. Because of the cobblestones and the loose babies, traffic crept; the pedestrians virtually ignored it, so that there was a vacation atmosphere. I used to go into the Siberia branch of the Chemical Bank for the fun of looking at who was assigned there. This was in a grotesquely ancient building across from a live poultry market and a garment ends warehouse, and the tellers were dazed from their banishment from Madison Avenue. Italian ices had been sold out of baby carriages by Puerto Ricans during the fall, and practically every block had its *shul.* A *shul* was a hole-in-the-wall synagogue with four or five Stars of David built into the front, looking defiant and jubilant, from some ghetto in Europe and bursting with hope. In the zany designs of a lot of the blocks you could see the failed architects who at last had been left a free hand; they sometimes went Moorish to celebrate. The neighborhood was as rich historically as the western range of the same period, but was being bulldozed away. I strolled and gazed through the misty weekends—at the patchworks of relic wallpaper on the sites half-demolished, at the washlines, the three downtown bridges—snacking on Old Country foods, and talking such talk as one enjoys slightly wistfully with a cab driver in more affluent years.

At the lab I tinked tunes on the urine bottles, lining them up. I treated the test frogs to beef liver for having been right about Ida from the start. Darwin was chiseling holes for a new wiring system. Five months instead of five years seemed the prognostication for him. He was eating graham crackers globbed with butter ("I can't stop") and got bigger and bigger, more like an overblown boy of fourteen. The woman whose door we left food at was also taking a turn for the worse. Twice she let her sink run until it overflowed. When we picked the lock we discovered her sitting in bed with her feet drawn up under her, watching the water. She creamed her skin and dyed her hair yellow, so it was hard to tell if she was senile or out of her mind.

I understood Darwin's fondness for mice. If you look at them they're graceful and comely. You can see them as panthers, you can see them as pandas. They cluck like a muffled henhouse, whereas guinea pigs sound like puppies down in the cellar. Light as a leaf and taut-legged, they skittered about their cages and sneezed from the bits of sawdust stirred up. They scratched their ears and cleaned their tails nattily and basked upon piles of each other as on piles of cushions, holding a nibble of food in their paws. Given food, they'd hurriedly wash their faces before feeling ready to eat, and when they were hunched on their hams, their shoulders bulged out like extra pouch cheeks. Their tails were their pride and spiritual spine; they always were handling them, bending them around to clean and inspect. Stiff, up-curved tails signaled a fight; or a nervous mouse, with kissing noises, vibrated his tail out stiff and straight. After endearing, midget yawns, they often slept in a row like suckling pigs, and pressed their paws against their cheeks. Or they burrowed head first in a pile so that just their fat rears and pink, bird legs and rubber-hose tails stuck out. As they sickened, their white tails zoned into gray; they sagged and wizened like little sand bags. Sometimes they fled death in leaps, so that it clenched them in mid-air and they thudded down. Sometimes they lay on their sides, scrubbing their noses in spasms and coughing and sneezing, and went rigid like that, rolled up in the pose in which they'd been born and scrubbing their pulsating nostrils. But it was generally a homey, humming room. Darwin and I often went in there.

My problems were solving themselves. If I was too scared to quit my job, the job was foundering under me. Obviously there would soon be no job. Although I was still at my window and my preoccupation with the violence got worse, I didn't dash down to the street so much. I avoided knots of the Harlem Negroes who worked near us, and I would break into sweats of fear at odd moments, walking through a dark block on the way home—I developed a whiz-along walk. The subway was more than ever like an armed camp and, when I came out, I would see everybody facing in one direction and a man there trying to box with a bus. One day a cement truck stopped revolving. Rather than funny it was frenetic. The driver cried. I'd gotten infallible at sensing a fight, sensing its start and exactly its course. Seeing people clumping in front of me, I'd usually turn off but sometimes I kept numbly on through the thick of it as if mesmerized.

The garage crowd amused itself by setting off leftover firecrackers from the horde they'd blackmarketed during the summer. They were having a lazy spell and would hire a passing bum to do some of their chores for a quarter or so. Ida was jumpy with me once our Christmas reunion was over, and Tony, taking his cue, was also cool. Yet we remained a threesome. He'd run away from me but when I caught him and lifted him up he hugged me even as he was struggling. Ida was furious at my treating her like a taboo object. She moved away as if not to let me touch her any time I came close. Although I couldn't conceive of sleeping with her after the suffering that we had gone through, her person still seemed as much mine as a wife's. I refused to stay out of her room when she dressed. I pinched her elbows to see what she weighed and if she was eating enough. I touched my tongue to her forehead if she looked pale to feel what her temperature was. I used to rub her whenever we talked—rubbed and rubbed. I'd spank or order her around, give gifts as usual, fondle and advise her son—everything except sleep with her. Now that her life wasn't a shambles, wasn't about to break apart, she was left with it, which was not very pleasant either. It was a precarious, temporary sort of friendship we had, both of us riding along until I would go my way.

January was uneventfully dreary. The boiler next door blew up and ours went on the blink for a week out of sympathy. One afternoon, at work, late again about six, I heard the electric horn blast, "You goddam spear-carrier!" A bum hadn't washed a car well enough but wanted his money. I winced at the window, it was all so familiar. The four mechanics were cutting across the lot in diagonal paths, toward the man or away after their monkey wrenches. The wife of the thin one was in the station, so he was trying to subdue his cousins a little, walking slower than them, waving his hand. The fellow was standing his ground on the theory that perseverance would carry him through. Standing quietly, he wasn't easy to see because his color just matched the shade of the darkness. His clothes showed up better. He was dead still. You had to look twice. He was only about in his forties, and everything happened very fast. When he saw the crowbars, he used language too. I was violently agitated. My face had lurched into a flinch; I'd stopped breathing. I was so clocked into the gears of this kind of stuff that every part of my body went sick as if as part of an allergy attack—I knew, I knew, I moved like one of the gears myself.

I was tearing downstairs. Outside, the whites were already in a half moon around the guy (the wife in the office door). "It was a shit, nigger job. You don't get nothing for that," said the blast-vigor brother with the voice like a highway horn. He had really too much energy to focus it on the one guy. The fat brother slouched in a posture of venom, but the muscle-bound hired man was less interested in hurting someone than in being strong. My lean opponent was between, holding them off as he cursed in an undertone for the Negro to run. In harassment he pointed at me as if "look what was coming."

"I done a good enough job. You weren't paying nothing but chicken feed anyhow. What do you want? You want to gyp me," said the man. He muttered that slavery wasn't going on any more. Not young, not quite humbled down into middle age, he was in the galled period of life when he had no impulsiveness left to save him. They encircled him, seeing how he took it, poking at his calves with a tire iron, and they called him one or two names. The auto trunks where they kept their weapons gaped open sinisterly. I'd drifted to the edge of the sidewalk on my side of the street with my tentative gait, my quick-backtrack gait, which had saved a great many necks by this time, including my own.

"I done a good job for you and you're going to keep my money?" He hadn't determined upon defiance, it was just happening. "What a poor sack of fish you are. You're cheapskates. Go on back to your tiddle-prick then. Go play with yourselves."

A moment went by before they could believe their ears. As one man, they turned and rushed for the woman, roaring, to drive her inside. The circle opened for that, but he still wasn't running; it was written into the lines of his body that he wasn't running. I'd never been faced with a situation where there was no running, so all my gingerly jumpiness was no help to me. I was picking my legs up and putting them down, twitching them almost like some sort of tail, but nevertheless remained frozen right where I was. I was nothing, unable to cross the street, unable to function. When they came back their feet shook the pavement, and a visible panic pushed up through his knees. The lean mechanic pointed at me to hold me where I was, and it was as though I were pressing against a thick pane of glass. The fellow did try to escape but had waited a second too long. They ran him into the wall and held him there tight, waving their shovels and irons. "Call the cops! Call the cops!" they were yelling to Musclebound, in order to establish that they had phoned first and that an attack on them by the Negro had followed Musclebound's call. He shoved a dime in the phone, beating on it. I could see the white faces like flowers behind me in our building's windows. It was closing time; most of the lights were off; the cobbler was getting into his coat. I think I was yelling—at least my mouth was open. The Negro had covered his face with his hands. Since he didn't try to dodge loose, they didn't hit him more than a couple of times. I was weeping with the collapse of my nerves and because I'd done nothing; I'd been unable even to move.

The police dispersed all of us, finally. I was shaking and finished with this. After spending a few days at home sleeping, drinking milkshakes, I called up an uncle of mine in the Midwest and borrowed enough to move uptown and devote myself to making a different start in the city.

VIOLENCE, VIOLENCE

AN ESSAY (1969)

I T IS CURIOUS THAT WITH such a crushing, befuddling climate of general violence as there is in New York we should still be paying money to go to the prizefights. The fight fan, as one used to picture him, was a kind of overweight frustrated homebody whose life was practically devoid of danger and drama. Middle-aged rather than young, a small businessman or a warehouse foreman, a nostalgic war veteran, he looked about and found the world torpid, so he came to St. Nicholas Arena to holler and twist on his folding chair, throw starts of punches, or did the same thing in front of the television set in a bar. But now this fellow has all the firepower of Vietnam on television, the racial-college riots, the hippies to hate, the burglaries in his building, the fear of being mugged when he is on the street. Going home from the prizefight, he runs a chance of being beaten up worse than the loser was. And boxing, which began as an all-out sport, has not been able to cinch its procedures tighter, the way pro football has done, to make for a more modish, high-strung commotion and wilder deeds. It's the simplest pageant of all: two men fight, rest a minute, and fight some more. Like the mile run, it's traditionalist and finite, humble in its claims.

Baseball, which seemed the natural man's sport above all, has turned out to be overly ceremonious and time-consuming for the 1960s, and even burlesque and the belly dancers of Eighth Avenue, forthright as we once supposed that they were, have been eclipsed by still more elementary displays of the human physique. The entrepreneurs of boxing didn't at first suspect that their sport had any kick left except as a TV filler for the hinterlands, where the old modes prevail. The custom of weekly

179

fights at St. Nick's or the old Garden had lapsed (since which, both buildings have gone *poof*). But then they tried a few cards at the National Maritime Union hiring hall, counting on the roughhouse seamen to provide a box-office backlog. When the shows sold out, they shifted them to the Felt Forum in the new Madison Square Garden and discovered that the sport pays there as well. As a result, live boxing has become a feature of New York life again. The problem of the promoters is not to streamline the *Geist* to fit the sixties but to find fighters who fight, because unlike many other athletes, prizefighters do not really enjoy their sport very much, as a rule; they fight for the purse. All our Irish and Italian citizens have elevated themselves until they don't have to choose between simonizing cars for a living or the prize ring, and the Negroes and Spanish-speakers too are scrambling upward toward better livelihoods, if only a campier sport with lots of legwork, like basketball, or the various ornate sports where if the team loses the coach loses his job. Boxing isn't like that, and we are bringing in hungry souls from Nigeria, the Philippines and the Bahamas to do the dirt. People sometimes make the mistake of feeling sorry for boxers, however, and want to abolish the sport, when they should look instead at the man in the neighborhood car wash who *isn't* a fighter—doesn't fly to Seattle for a big card—but runs the steam hose and polishes fenders.

And is it dirt? I'm not one of those professional eyewitnesses who is willing to watch anything just on the grounds that it is happening. I live on Ambulance Alley and don't need to go to the Garden in order to see men in desperate straits. I go to admire a trial of skills, a contest of limited violence between unintimidated adversaries which, even when it does spill out of the ring after a bad decision and the crowd in its anger sways shoulder to shoulder, is very nineteenth-century, from the era of cart horses in the street. Every sport is a combat between its participants, but boxing is combat distilled, purer even than combat with weapons. When a referee steps in and stops a fight in which one man is receiving punishment without any hope of recouping, the crowd is not disappointed at seeing the punishment stopped; they are glad enough about that. If they are disappointed, it's because the drama is over, which was true as soon as the fight became one-sided. Boxing's appeal is its drama and grace, a blizzarding grace that amounts to an impromptu, exigent ballet, especially in the lighter and nimbler weights. Hands, arms, feet, legs, head, torso—more is done per moment than in fast ice hockey; and since there is more motion, the athletes in other sports cannot surpass a consummate boxer for grace.

Still, why this extra violence? Is it choreographed like a bullfight; is it like a fine tragedy which one goes to although one's own life is tangled enough? Of course it isn't these things at all. There is no program, no unity, no meaning as such unless a parable fortuitously develops, and the spectators are there for the combat. Writers of the Hemingway-Mailer axis have been fascinated by the combat, locating relevancies and identities in the pre-fight rituals, but they have not made claims for the sport as an art. Ten years ago, when we did not live alongside such an ocean of violence, some of us went to the fights perhaps as one keeps an aquarium. We realized that most of the world was under water, but we were high and dry with Eisenhower, and knowing that life is salt and life is action, life is tears and life is water, we kept a fish tank to represent the four-fifths of the world which breathed with gills.

But nowadays we're flooded and swimming for dear life, no matter where we happen to live. That we nevertheless prefer our sports violent—the irreducible conciseness of boxing—is evidence of a relation to violence, a need and a curiosity, so basic that it cannot be sated. Though we do tire of the delirium in the streets, we are only tiring of the disorder. Make it concise, put ropes or white lines around it, and we will go, we will go, just as people on vacation go down to the roaring sea.